M000047075

Prairie Schooner Book Prize in Fiction | Editor: Kwame Dawes

EXTINCTION EVENTS

Liz Breazeale

UNIVERSITY OF NEBRASKA PRESS | LINCOLN

© 2019 by the Board of Regents of
the University of Nebraska

Acknowledgments for the use of copyrighted
material appear on page 121, which constitute
an extension of the copyright page.

Library of Congress Cataloging-in-Publication Data
Names: Breazeale, Liz, author.
Title: Extinction events: stories / Liz Breazeale.
Description: Lincoln: University of Nebraska Press,
2019. | Series: Prairie Schooner Book Prize in Fiction
Identifiers: LCCN 2019003681
ISBN 9781496215628 (pbk.: alk. paper)
ISBN 9781496218308 (epub)
ISBN 9781496218315 (mobi)
ISBN 9781496218322 (pdf)
Classification: LCC PS3602.R4325 A6
2019 | DDC 813/.6—dc23
LC record available at https://lccn.loc.gov/2019003681

Set in Janson by E. Cuddy.
Designed by N. Putens.

For my parents

CONTENTS

ACKNOWLEDGMENTS

I have always written, but I owe an inescapably deep debt of gratitude to the teachers and professors who helped me evolve into a writer. Thank you to my first creative writing professors at Missouri State University: Jen Murvin, Shannon Wooden, and W. D. Blackmon. You were the first to take me seriously and teach me how to craft.

To my professors and cohort at Bowling Green State University: Without your insight, writing wisdom, and fierce generosity, the stories in this collection would not exist. Thank you for taking a chance on a young woman from southwest Missouri who had a whole lot of messy talent and very little fine-tuning, and thank you for teaching me how to be a writer. To Lawrence Coates and Wendell Mayo: You gave nothing but encouragement and advice, and you always brought out my best work with your questions and insight.

When I joined the master's program, I was constantly told to find "my people," the ones who understood my work. To Laura and Jackie: We found each other! Without your insightful critiques, your honesty, and your constant unflinching support, I wouldn't have finished many of the stories I've written, much less this entire book. What started as a Winter Wheat panel has become a deep and meaningful friendship I cannot do justice to in these few sentences, but what I do have the space to say is that I am a better writer and person because of you both. To Lauren, Chelsea, and Jenelle: You are amazing women and incredible poets, and I'm so privileged to have you as friends. I learned so much from each of you, including how not to open a bottle of wine with a shoe and a pen.

Thank you to Carmen Toussaint and the lovely writers at Rivendell

Writers' Colony, with whom I spent an incredible two weeks. You gave me the space, time, and solitude to hone the final stories in this manuscript as well as motivating, fascinating evenings of fellowship, conversation, and way too much wine.

Thank you a hundred times over to Kwame Dawes, Bernice McFadden, and Jack Driscoll, for choosing *Extinction Events* over so many brilliant manuscripts. Thank you to Ashley Strosnider at *Prairie Schooner* and Courtney Ochsner at the University of Nebraska Press for making this process painless and easy.

My biggest thank you of all: To my parents and sister, for almost thirty years of undying support. I owe everything to my parents, who fostered a deep and abiding love of literature in me and who never once told me to find a more sensible career path. To Grammy: Thank you for being my first editor all those years ago and writing down every single story I made up and dictated to you. Thank you also to various family members who acted out the plays I made up as a child and who still encourage me to this day.

Finally, thank you, thank you to the journals who first published the following stories:

Pleiades: "Un-Discovered Islands"
Nashville Review: "Four Self-Portraits of the Mapmaker"
Passages North: "Survival in the Plague Years"
Territory: "The Lemurians"
Booth: "Extinction Events Proposed by My Father"
Sou'wester: "The Disaster Preparedness Guidebook"
Arroyo Review: "How Cities Are Lost"
Flyway: "Devil's Tooth Museum"
Tupelo Quarterly: "The Supernova of Irvin Edwards"
The Carolina Quarterly: "Ashcake"
Sycamore Review: "Experiencers"

EXTINCTION EVENTS

1

Un-Discovered Islands

The first island to disappear was barely land at all.

My fourteen-year-old daughter discovers the clickbait one evening: They Look for This Island, But What They Find Instead Will Blow Your Mind.

I peek over her shoulder as she narrates: Apparently a research vessel on its way to New Zealand noticed Midge Island, a speck of reef, was not where the map said it should be, was, in fact, nowhere at all.

My husband scoffs. Don't read that garbage. He is splayed across the loveseat, laptop resting on his thighs. He continues: This kind of thing used to happen when people drew maps by hand, and these tiny sandbars or whale corpses or kelp rafts, they kept being copied forward because nobody questioned it.

I google Midge Island.

My daughter scrolls on. Her voice holds a wave, a minor tremble, when she speaks. It's gone, though. That's what it says. Midge Island just disappeared.

That doesn't sound real, kiddo.

Mom, were you tracking it?

My graduate students and I chart islands impacted by climate change, the rate of erosion for each coastline, estimating the amount of time before they are devoured by the sea.

I've never heard of it.

Don't encourage this, says my husband. He swivels, catches his laptop before it falls. Islands don't just disappear.

I zoom in on a satellite map, expecting a grain of sand in a rolling blue Pacific eye. But there's only empty ocean, a patch of skin from which a scar has faded or a birthmark has been removed.

My daughter plants herself further back into the couch cushion, tapping at her phone. She has always chosen words carefully, scientifically. When she was younger she saw a spider once, hesitated before stomping it out. She said, I was terrified. No, petrified.

She asks, so it's happened before?

Sailors used to get confused in the 1800s, my husband says. Drunk. Sometimes they saw things that weren't there.

My daughter looks so young in this moment. I want to promise her that it's nothing to worry about, that Midge Island has never existed so it couldn't disappear.

It's nothing, says my husband.

But a thought is germinating, a gritty thought, too impossible to speak, a foreboding like being alone in a darkened street.

In the morning my daughter's face is all rocky shore, all treacherous reef and sweeping tide. My husband asks how she is and all she says is fine, barely looking up from her unfinished geometry homework. I have coffee with a colleague about a book we are writing and my husband forgets his lunch and I do not think of Midge Island again. Its most recognizable quality is that it is no longer here.

Kiribati vanishes one week later, a periwinkle and golden paradise, a flower petal archipelago strung across the sea.

We were tracking this one, I tell my husband. Kiribati is number one on internet lists of Top Ten Most Beautiful Remote Islands and Ten Gorgeous Islands You Need to Visit ASAP Before Climate Change Destroys Them.

So it was erosion, he says, leaning over my shoulder, hard plastic of his glasses against my temple.

No, not this quickly.

I was interviewed once for a well-known science podcast, a live show, alongside a climatologist from Kiribati, a woman who answered questions in front of an audience with more ease than I can ever pull off. I spoke about ocean levels, the ways we are always being eroded. The scientist from Kiribati described the situation for her country, its atolls always under siege, each tide rising higher than the last.

The male host nodded as we spoke, interrupting and questioning and scooping the ends of our sentences under the beginnings of his own, our thoughts and words becoming only sand swept out to sea. He did it while the other woman was discussing her peoples' likely future evacuation, then started to ask what could be done. She cut him off.

She said, we won't let ourselves be eroded. You can't disappear us.

My husband has stepped away from the desk now, massed himself across the room. They had a language, he says. Have. They have a whole language.

He specializes in dying languages, is convinced we will lose the power to communicate before we go extinct. It panics him so much, this idea, that he began correcting my daughter's grammar as soon as she started to speak, her eyes going wide as he told her, It's *I want*, not just want. *I want.*

Want, said my daughter. She couldn't quite shape it, the I.

He shakes his head. This has to be a mistake.

In the same way he pauses over vicious comments like the ones I receive with every op-ed I publish, in the same way he clears his throat. In the same way he responded to a boy pulling our daughter's ponytail years ago at school with, boys will be boys.

My husband once more says, someone has made a mistake. He looks past me like he is trying to see some unknown intact land.

A small island called North Sentinal is gone on a Wednesday. It was home to one of the only untouched tribes in the world. We first read the news at work, a colleague and I, and he shrugged. No one could go there, he said, so wasn't it always lost?

I didn't respond, and later that evening, when I tell my husband over the sound of wine bottle on glass, he shakes his head. Jesus, he says, what do you even say to that?

He is smiling, an awkward half-smile, and drops of wine mark his lips. There is a glassiness to his gaze, a melting into light, an air like a beam through fog, like he is trying to pierce a haze he cannot understand.

All the reports say it just disappeared. Like the other ones. Like—

Disappeared sounds too easy, he continues. He is galloping through words, through sentences, the way he did when his mother died, when his anxiety becomes greater than his care for language. Disappeared sounds like someone wiped them away in the night. Like they never existed.

Neither of us teach in the morning, had planned to work after dinner, but when we see the news of North Sentinal, my husband's disbelief blossoms into anxiety, an unease that settles throughout each room.

We need a word for these islands, we need something new, we need something better.

He uses the word "we" like the two of us are automatically united in his quest, just as he did when I told him I was pregnant. He still has no idea that I waited two weeks to tell him. He never asked when I had known. He just assumed the knowledge was his, his and mine, immediately.

Extinct, he says, pouring another glass.

Absent, I reply, humoring him.

Lost.

Un-discovered. It rolls from my mouth, a tripping word. A hyphenated pause, a skip in a record, like the moment when the doctor asked, do you want to hear the heartbeat? And I almost thought I might say no, the repelling, the recoiling, captured in that breath.

Shit, says my husband. Okay. I deserve partial credit here.

It's not a kid. You didn't half-raise it.

At the doctor my husband said, let's hear our child.

I couldn't say it, could only say: Mine. My body.

My husband gulps the last of his wine.

When North Sentinal was first discovered by outsiders years ago, the North Sentinalese made it clear they didn't want contact. This is ours, they signaled. This is ours.

It took the men from outside ages to understand, until they were pelted by Sentinalese arrows, Sentinalese spears.

Tristan da Cunha is un-discovered four days later.

It had a United Kingdom post code. The people could order packages from Amazon.

I am asked to be on CNN for a Skype interview.

Why me, I ask. I'm not famous.

Well, says the person on the line, we know of your books. You're "erosion famous."

I tell my husband later that night.

He tells me I will be fantastic, pauses before saying, but they're just disappearing. They're not eroding.

Un-discovering, you mean.

A flash of grin, a leaning away.

I clean the office before the interview. My husband tries to help, but he is constantly asking where something should go, what he should do next. There's too much detritus to clear away completely—papers and folders and books and a few tiny insect corpses, desiccated and crumpling into themselves—so I shove everything behind the desk, under the futon.

The interview starts and the host asks, so you know the subject of erosion like the back of your hand, can you give us your ideas here?

I talk about climate change. I talk about how the ocean is chipping away at everything.

But this isn't erosion, says the anchor. These islands are going away out of nowhere. So what would you call that?

It's like they're being un-discovered. Like the opposite of finding.

Un-discovered, says the anchor. He savors the word, lets it trickle from his lips. That's perfect.

Later, after congratulating me, my husband nods at the screen. He says, look. You're trending.

The ticker reads: Senator says un-discovered islands brought this on themselves.

Turn it off, says my daughter. She stares at him, takes him into a gaze that is an eruption forming a crust, new land through which he cannot crack.

My husband, glancing from her to me, says, it's scary, I know, kiddo.

She spins on him, eyes wide and dark, just like mine. I'm not a kid.

I'm just saying, we're all scared.

You don't understand, she shouts over her shoulder, punctuating the final word with her footsteps as she sprints upstairs.

Teenagers. My husband shakes his head. I'll go talk to her.

But I am out of the kitchen before he can move.

My daughter only lets me in her room after I promise I'm alone.

It takes her ages, eons, to finally shake her head when I ask if she's okay.

There is a new drinking game, apparently. You name islands, she tells me, you all name islands one by one, places that might disappear next. You drink while you think. Or you drink when you can't think of anything. It depends.

I do not want my child playing this game. Somehow the game is more terrifying than the alcohol. When she was born I had the sense of wearing my organs outside of my body, of being boneless and skinless and unprotected. I did not understand it, how she could be herself but also a little of me too.

When you run out of islands, she says, you just start saying places.

One of her friends was playing at a party over the weekend. When she passed out, boys pulled away her clothes, took pictures of her.

That's all, she says, as though this is not enough, as though she has no right to be upset.

She pauses before saying, they call her Midge now. Because there's nothing left to see.

I hear in her voice a lightness I understand, that comes from losing yourself, the sand grains, the glassy sparkling particles of you, swept away a little every time a man screams at you from a car or touches you without asking or tells you without telling you how the world is not yours. I do not want her to lose the feel of a new dress before men see her in it or the texture of new lipstick before men taste it, before it bloodies their lips like they are biting out parts of her. I want to weigh her down, keep her from floating away in the tide, but I know it has already begun.

My husband comes to her room to apologize and she accepts, graceful, and it frightens me, the veneer girls wear from so young, the ease with which men are forgiven.

I tell my husband about it later, the photographs, the girl's clothes peeled away like layers of sunburnt skin.

He cannot believe it. We've met those boys, he says. They're good kids, aren't they? That's someone's daughter.

I send an email to the school. She's a person, I say.

Only it comes out like a plea.

When Svalbard is un-discovered, it plays on every twenty-four-hour news channel. The Global Seed Vault was there, a safe house for the world's genetic diversity, a gray building thrust through the ice, a bland but valuable monster.

I am on CNN again, talking heads with a man who can only loosely be described as a journalist. Actually, he says, the real question is, why aren't we looking into alternative theories? For instance, the fact that some of these islands have never been listed on maps.

I find myself preaching caution when all I can think is, did you not know? Did you not know that the world can fall apart?

Some people think it's aliens, the journalist insists. Some people think it's God. Some people think it's the Earth, breaking apart slowly. Should we be listening to them? It sounds like you all know the same amount.

The sentence hangs, the way fog does in a valley.

I've studied erosion my whole adult life, I reply. Or maybe since before then, maybe since I was born.

What's erosion got to do with this?

I have a sense of vertigo, not with height but with time, standing on the verge of myself at this moment, gazing at all the other moments that have come before, unable to pick out the strata of them, the moments of my life and who I was before now; they are all too molten, too volcanic. Who I was before my college boyfriend fucked me so painfully I gave him blowjobs so I would not have to sleep with him, who I was before I had this child, who I was before my husband, before the maternity leave left me frustrated and empty.

It's the study of disappearing, I say.

We argue for a few moments more before the interview ends.

Later that night I can't sleep. I find my daughter in the den, rigid and blanketed, clutching her knees to her chest like the mummies they find on the tops of mountains. She is perfectly preserved, her face awash in the colors of un-discovery. History channels are airing specials about lost cities and I wonder if they are meant to be comforting, these images of stonework erupting from jungles, statues awakening through vines. If they're all saying, we've lost things before, but see, we find them again.

I watched one of these the other night, I tell her. About phantom islands, islands that turn out to be mirages or dead whales or hallucinations.

I know what they are.

Of course she does. She already knows about diminishing, about curling herself into a shell.

We're always losing stuff, she whispers.

I feel that she is waiting, waiting for her mother to make sense of something. To tell her that the world is not terrifying, not to me, and because she is partly me, mostly me, all me, that one day it will cease to be terrifying for her. That she will never catch her breath walking alone, that she will lose nothing.

But when I sit next to her we do not speak. The sofa creaks as she lays her head on my shoulder. The heaviness does not come from weight.

The world is emptying and constricting all at once, like water through a closing fist.

We hold our monthly book club out of some strange defiance, some deep-down female anger. None of us has even brought the novel.

Our phones all buzz at once, the same tone shocking the air as the one used for Amber Alerts, the tone we all understand to mean that something has been lost, something that must be recovered at all costs. There is a collective breath.

Someone whispers, shit.

One of my colleagues turns to me. You went there once, didn't you? Easter Island?

Yes, I reply. It is all a blur now, like trying to pick out one tree in a landscape of trees, trying to focus on it, to memorize it, all from the window of a moving car.

My daughter used one of my photos of a moai as a model for one she made in sixth grade. We pored over my photo album to find the right one.

She asked, what were you doing there?

The hills, balding and fuzzy with infant grasses. The wind, how it screamed. The profound loneliness of the moai, their always-open eyes, their sense of having watched civilizations slough away.

We were studying, I told her. The way the environment weathered the island. The way it's been picked apart.

I watched my daughter giggling at my outdated outfits. I watched her and I thought that from the moment she was born the world was narrowing around her, was squeezing and saying you fit so well just here, do not move, you can be whatever you want as long as it is motionless.

Everyone at book club has heard about the drinking game. I owned a stab of silent pleasure earlier in the evening, a guilty hit of smugness when the others said things like, oh, it was like pulling teeth to get Shawn to talk to me. We shook our heads at the unfortunate incident—as some mothers said—with my daughter's friend, so long ago, a half hour ago, when we thought we could attempt to be normal again. We talked about how strangely terrifying this drinking game was, the adaptability of our children.

After Easter Island, though, none of us want to leave. Either we do not want to end this evening, this one night away from our families, or we have had too much wine, or we are keeping at bay something that is nameless and dark and always with us but seems to fade when we are in the company of other women.

It is only a matter of time, then, before one of us starts the drinking game.

New Zealand.

Pitcairn Island.

Kelleys Island.

We cannot think of islands.

Peru.

Zimbabwe.

Tampa.

That's just where you were born, I scold.

It is dizzying, this new game, this new world. I do not want my daughter to understand that even places we have touched and in which we have existed, those things we believe to be eternal and unchanging, can now be gone entirely without warning. I do not want her to play this game or drink alcohol or have children, to carry them and give them to this world like she is giving a part of herself, a part she never really knew.

Kalamazoo.

Brooklyn.

That's your name, someone says. Brooklyn is who you are.

We are breathless, giggling. We are staggering. We are all touching one another, palm to backbone or arm to arm, anything to say, I am still here. I am still Brooklyn, I am still Katy, I am still Margaret. I am a person, I am existing, I am not un-discovered.

Here are the theories that appear on CNN, post–Easter Island:

Fractured ocean theory, which posits that the seas are parting, swallowing each island.

Who Cares? The leader of this movement believes the end is near anyway, so why bother.

Aliens. This one has no real name, but a man who calls himself an Ancient Alien Theorist explains that they are coming back. For what? He's not sure.

The world fragments. One of my students is dropping out. She tells me this in person, her husband standing outside my office door. When I ask her why, she says, I have my family to think about. I see her two days later, obscured by her husband and children, walking into a church. The sign reads, hopes and prayers for the un-discovered.

More theories are given more air time. Magnetism. Satan/Demons. An angry God. Many angry gods.

A man murders his wife for refusing to join the Church of the Disappearance, a new Christian sect that believes the un-discovered people have been raptured.

She's always laughing at me, says the man to police. She always says I'm so stupid.

Just before the president makes a joint announcement with the Canadian prime minister—she, exhausted, and he, boyish at forty—a man is caught scaling the White House fence with an assault rifle. As he is carted away he screams about that bitch, that bitch is going to disappear us all.

It is always men who say these things, always men who form these cults, these bizarre conspiracies.

Well, says my husband, not all men.

The president and the prime minister go on with their address about the refugees, a mixture of those desperate to leave islands that still exist and those left abroad when their homes were un-discovered. There are thousands and thousands of them, and Canada and the

United States pledge to help as many as possible. My daughter watches the president, flushed with admiration.

But she is asked, inevitably, about the intruder. Weary, the president says, the thing about being a woman is, you get used to people wanting to kill you.

She shouldn't have said that, snaps my husband.

It's true, says my daughter.

Don't talk like that.

Of course she should, I tell him.

It's like they can't handle it. The simple reality of constant fear.

The next day Hawaii is un-discovered.

School is canceled for the rest of the week and universities are closed. We sit in the living room and watch the president drop a wreath into the ocean where the big island once was. Her face is empty, an abyssal plain.

My daughter asks, is Hawaiian a dead language now?

Dying, at least. My husband's face is being engulfed by dark circles; he has started writing in the night about the languages that have disappeared. He always says that word, too, never un-discovered.

My husband takes my daughter's hand and says, we're not going to disappear. His voice is staticky, like he is being patched through a radio.

But my daughter and I exchange a glance. I understand that she already knows, and she has the eyes of someone older.

She slips her hand from her father's.

She is all tremor. What do they call it when people are un-discovered?

I don't know, I say.

But I do, and she does.

All international flights are canceled. No airline wants a repeat of Hawaii, when planes were forced into emergency landings. One or two crashed into the ocean, but no one talks about them.

The captain of the international space station gives an interview, is asked how this looks from space, if they can see it happen, anything at all. Weightless, she and a male officer constantly bump one another in a way that would otherwise be comical. He is gripping her arm, steadying himself. The look passing across the captain's face is a shimmer, a ripple of something like hate. I know this expression, know how it has to be wrangled, controlled.

I am asked to be on CNN again. We like your sense of humor, they tell me.

I should tell them that I can't give them any answers. I should tell them I've been to Easter Island and I've been to Hawaii and don't know how it is that they've stopped existing, how it is that I am no longer the person who has been to either of those places, not anymore.

But I don't. I tell them, oh, that's nice.

Although I can't imagine how anything could possibly be funny again, my daughter latched to the couch next to my husband, a mussel clinging to a rock, watching the tide pull away. Above them we hang, suspended in our photo frame.

The Skype interview begins with the anchor saying, I mean, it's Hawaii, like he cannot quite form the words. Hawaii is gone now.

It begs the question, says the man on the other line, about whether any of these places are real. Have they even existed?

I know Hawaii was real, I say. I think, wow. I had to say that on live TV.

Whoever is on the other line argues with this. Somehow we have reached a point where a real human is taking issue with my stance on Hawaii. How do I know, he asks. I've never been. How do I know it was real?

Thankfully the office is littered with photo albums. I hold one up, one with a flowery cover that my daughter gave me for a birthday. I've been there, I say. I point to the first page, a photograph of the three of us standing in front of a palm tree.

You could be in Barbados. You could be in St. Thomas.

I flip the pages. Here's me and my husband. Here's my kid snorkeling.

They're beautiful, says the anchor.

They are beautiful, those people. Those phantom people on their phantom island.

Nothing happens for a full month, a glacial time span. The kids go back to school, my husband and I go back to work; the news begins to air stories on missing hikers or the resurgence of Lyme disease. My daughter sleeps through the night, her face brightening once more. People throw parties and get married and begin to take deep breaths, begin to realize that we have been afraid to exhale. Memorial days are added to the calendar—Un-Discovery Days. Even Midge Island has one. We, the ones still here, the lucky ones, throw ourselves into reality with the force of people who have escaped some great trauma.

But there is a deep loss in the air. I feel it all the time, an electric background hum, the dull existence of an undiagnosed pain.

We go out to dinner and the restaurant is packed, seething with people. I'd forgotten how the world is full, overflowing with humanity.

My husband toasts, desperate. I think it might be over, he says.

What if it's not? My daughter has not raised her water glass, her hand lingering over her knife and fork.

Cheer up. We're still here.

But I understand. What if we're not here, not completely. What if we've been lost, un-discovered along the way. In touchings that linger too long, with words and the lack of them and emptinesses and feelings that have no articulations—only colors like the color an object leaves after we close our eyes, spangly and moving into darkness, only the sense of inertia stalled over a missing piece.

Tell her, hon. Tell her it's okay now.

But I can only rub my daughter's back. I can only hope that the lack of space between us is enough.

On the way home the Breaking News chime sounds on the radio.

It is an automated message, has been since Easter Island. It takes a toll, I suppose, reading over and over one word, two words, containing in them the endings of lives.

Be advised, says the voice.

My daughter tenses against the seat.

Please be advised that as of eight o'clock Central Standard Time the island of New Zealand has been un-discovered.

Fuck, says my husband.

Please be advised, the radio tells us.

My daughter is a ghost in the rearview mirror, dissipating.

Please be advised.

I wonder if the person behind that new voice had to record the name of every single island. Every single country, every single continent, every single landmass.

Indonesia and Ireland are un-discovered the next day. My husband does not want us to leave the house. He watches the chyron on CNN.

Costa Rican riots continue.

Chunnel closed as millions march from England.

Australian PM urges calm.

Environmentalists fear mass extinctions.

Cult leader promises all un-discovered people have been born again: All you have to do is find them.

How nice it would be to find them again, the un-discovered parts of the world. How easy, to make ourselves whole.

Two days later there is a meeting at my daughter's school. The principal insists that it will be good to feel normal, as though we have not shifted to a new normal where terror is constant and now suddenly real because men feel it too.

We're not going, says my husband. He only takes his eyes off the TV to scrawl something down. We have to stay here.

We can't just sit at home all day.

What world are you living in? It's not safe out there.

The passed-out girl and the photographs and the staying in and the going out and the losing and the gaining—when has it ever been safe?

I'll go, says my daughter.

Like hell you will.

He's standing now, my husband, body like an iceberg.

I nod. Of course we'll go.

You're not taking my daughter out there.

I had a C-section when my daughter was born and it didn't hurt but I felt everything, and this is how I feel now—like parts of me are being removed, like my body is being un-discovered from inside out.

I want to articulate this to my husband, I want to find the words because the words would give him solace, maybe, could bridge the chasm of the two worlds in which we live, but there are no words for this feeling that he could understand, the feeling of all the hollows of yourself collapsing into one.

You can't leave me, he says.

My daughter turns, walks away.

Only for a little while, I tell him. He turns the TV louder. He is drowning the silence we leave behind.

My daughter and I do not speak the entire drive.

When we enter the auditorium there is only a male voice, echoey and weak.

My daughter leads the way down the aisle, forces me in her wake. I see her shimmery, collapsing around the edges.

It is all women, clustered at the foot of the stage around a small TV on a cart. The anchor hesitates, his terror visible through the screen—the whites of his eyes, the streaks of his makeup.

Japan, he says. That is all he can manage, gaping at his female cohost.

I almost start to laugh at him, this man who cannot talk about un-discovery, about the ending of the world.

All he can say is, Japan.

Indonesia, says one of the mothers.

Australia.

New Zealand.

New Zealand is already gone, says my daughter, stepping back, the warmth of her against me.

There are no more islands, replies another mom.

We must all be drunk from a loss, from many losses, because we cannot name them or speak them and they sit in the back of our throats and maybe they always have.

Brooklyn.

I wonder if she means the place or her name.

Louisa.

Rachel.

I am a water droplet clinging, being shaken free.

Marianne.

Julie.

My daughter is opening her mouth and speaking her name and I reach for myself, any part of me I might recognize. I reach for beaches, reach for shores, reach for trees, reach for land. I am floating right there, right where the islands are supposed to be. I am reaching for something solid but finding only ocean.

2

Four Self-Portraits of the Mapmaker

1. New World

As a girl she draws worlds in her own image, tattoos maps like the mothwing parchment is her skin, like the lines and borders she sketches are meridians of bone, azimuths of hair, zenith eyes. She cannot name it, this marrow-deep pulse, this continental drift that leads her to sketch this way, to knit her scattered plates together in some volcanic shuffle, the healing of some broken bone under her surface.

The mapmaker's mother sometimes works from the floor with her, writing church hymns, setting lyrics to tunes that are not her own, scratching out straight-backed letters, an expedition of words traveling nowhere, discovering nothing. She traces her finger over the mapmaker's sketches, says they are lovely, but absently and hovering, a hummingbird searching for a sturdier space to land. The mapmaker feels that she has a chapel of a mother, meek and still and full of others.

Her father arrives, reaches for her drawings. Angles them, spins them, peers behind. This must be the Holy Land, he proclaims, all pulpit voice, which resounds as though from the prow of a ship.

She shrugs. It's not anywhere.

Her mother says, maybe this is Australia.

She considers what it would mean to translate her map and whether she even could.

It's not a map if nobody can read it. Her father snatches the pen. He boxes off a corner of the page.

This line, make it a continent border. And this, a country.

Until they are claw marks in a soft vast underbelly. Until she feels them under her skin, lacerating the heart of her made concrete.

I knew what they meant, she says, voice silken and quivering from her mouth like a snake's tongue, testing the air and her father and this space, where she is told instead of asked.

Her father laughs and her mother hesitates, before she does too. You just needed help.

She looks at the ruined map with its shipwreck letters and feels lost at sea. She lifts the pen, tries once more to render herself into an earth, her jetties of limbs into coasts, scars into landmarks. She tries but now her lines scab over remnants, indents of her father's marks like bites, like imprints that cannot be erased.

2. Dragons

In high school art class the mapmaker devours travelogues and the journals of explorers and centuries-old maps. The boy who sits across from her sometimes compliments her work; when he speaks her face pools with a volcanic heat, a magma she cannot control.

She sketches the endless ocean, her body folded over plains of the Midwest, sheets of Antarctic ice, the voids of the world that she can fill with dragons. Whenever she finds spaces that swirl with sawgrass or snow or jawbone waves, she places a dragon there, roaring or howling or snarling, protecting something she cannot name or draw.

She looks to the boy across the table, who stops his own drawing of a pear-shaped dog to say, those dragons are pretty sweet. Sometimes they laugh about something a classmate has said and they always warm her, these interactions, before he spins to his friends seated next to him.

That night she draws a new map, thinks of the boy with the lopsided smile who looks at her as if he understands, as if he could plot her across charts and pages without effort.

The next day in class, heart pounding tidal forces against the pinkness of her skin, the mapmaker smiles and hands the boy her creation.

What's this?

The mapmaker's gut pitches and yaws and the dragons glare.

It's nothing, she says. Just, you said you liked the dragons, so I drew some for you.

Oh, he says. I guess that's cool.

The mapmaker cannot quite get it out, the description she has in her mind, of how the dragons, ferocious and angry, exist to protect something unexplored and unnamed, something not yet formed. She tells him the old mapmakers used dragons to mark unknown territories, places they did not understand.

Thank you. He blinks. That's nice.

When she sees him stuff the map in his bag and whisper shut up to his friend her eyes scald and she wishes she could throw away the jetsam of her skin and her body, could sail away light and unencumbered.

She draws more dragons that night, so many they seem to multiply across wildernesses and seas. Monsters with features like her own—a flash of angry eye, a cheekbone become spiked tail. Scales shaped like fingernails. Mouths clustered with glacial jagged teeth.

3. Survey

After college she plots geological survey data on maps.

She tells her boss she loves this, translating the world into a readable text, an intimate conversation.

He laughs. Jesus. Translating is for languages.

For her first project she is to spool lines, colors, elevations and depths. She is to provide core information for a drilling firm to find areas of weakness and strength, presence and absence. She asks the man at the next cubicle if he has any paper and he holds up a yellow legal pad.

Good paper, I mean.

You an artist or something?

She finds the paper in a supply closet under a single crusty rubber glove and a chalky sponge. The paper is coarse, faded bile yellow, swarmed with water stains.

The pencil sags into the page and smudges at her touch, but the landscape, the lines, can still hold some of her, can still twist and loop in ways she herself moves or thinks or feels.

She reveals the map to her boss when he asks how the project is going.

He rubs his eyes. Christ, he almost shouts.

I always draw first.

He takes the pen from his pocket, slashes away entire quadrants. You're supposed to use this software first. And last. And always. He glowers over the cubicle wall at the man, says, you're her project manager. You let her waste time like this?

She speaks before she can stop the words. I just did it. Nobody let me.

It won't happen again, says the man, standing, moving toward the mapmaker, chest toward their boss like he is shielding her from some assault. Won't happen again. I'll explain to her.

When the boss stalks away, the man leans over and apologizes.

I understand, Project Manager. She turns on her computer, screen throwing glares and shapes without form into her own reflection, distorting everything.

Working with the program is painful. The apexes and vertices mismatch, the lines harsh and deep, too visible, devouring the area she maps. The dots become ticks, draining the pools of empty space until all is grid and block. She fears what her boss will growl next; to her the contours skew, wild vessels straying off track, and the coordinates strand too far apart. She sighs often and when she is silent her Project Manager calls, everything okay? in a singsong that becomes sharp, knuckles on a frozen window, rapping into her concentration.

When she hands the map to her boss he nods. See? Wasn't so hard. Good work, hon.

She says nothing to her boss and nothing to the man who eyes her all the way back to her desk, where she reworks her original, the one sketched by hand. She cannot erase the toxic black streaks. She tries to sketch dragons but they are less fierce, less like her—sandy, eroded, shapes without definition or spine.

4. Failed Expeditions

The man in the next cubicle calls himself a cartographer, a linear, sterile word she laughs at. They eat at foreign restaurants where the air is spice and clamor. In bookstores he points out places he's been, glances at her until she grins or remarks. Sometimes they speak the same words at the same time and it is like tracing landscapes on a snowy blank page.

He watches her draw, watches the maps blossom, marvels at her elegance. He says one morning, I told my parents about your maps. My dad would love for you to draw the town where they met. For their anniversary.

She smiles and says she'll think about it, but with a sense of loss, as though a knot has come undone.

The mapmaker charts him in her mind, his tropics and doldrums, delineations of spine and limb she surveys with her lips, tongue, fingers. He becomes the projection by which she plots her life; she triangulates her day and her night, tracking herself by every time he tugs her like he is a tide and the mountain of him in her thoughts and the time he says, don't you think that lipstick is too bright?

He asks her one night, would you have been an explorer? You know, way back?

She pictures her father and mother, how one of them is always the discoverer and the other always the discovered. Absolutely, she responds. First woman to the North Pole. Along the way I'd find the Northwest Passage.

I hate the cold.

Explorers always need someone to write them encouraging letters from home.

Why not go somewhere we both like?

She shakes her head at the sputter creeping under his voice. I've always wanted to travel by sled.

You'd leave me, wouldn't you? Just leave me behind so you could die of hypothermia.

I'd find Franklin's frozen corpse and bring you back his hand. You'd become very popular because of your amazing souvenirs.

His tone withers, chills. I don't have a girlfriend so I can be lonely.

She tries to stir him from his sudden sulk. It's not like I'd leave you for a walrus or anything.

But you'd leave.

She throws up her hands and turns on the television. He props his feet on the coffee table and crosses his arms and the room is cold and barren.

Soon she finds herself ignoring these questions or lying when she answers, so his body stays rainforest warm next to her. She fears her answers to his hypotheticals will drive her from him, will open vast new wilds uncertain and empty.

She tries to feel him as an astrolabe, guiding her home, because she fears she is a passage marked for someone else's exploration. Her maps are breathless, failed expeditions, closed routes and cairnless peaks and savage empty corridors from which no one returns.

She aches to exorcise them, these haunted fruitless journeys, so she picks up her pen, begins to map a sense of something lost, a land long left behind.

When she tells him it is for his parents, he stands behind her, suggests this estuary or this island or this cape.

She cannot help but wonder as he hovers if her magnetic north has shifted. They feel the same way about movies and books except when they don't and he jokes that she is wrong and tells her why.

They both want to travel and they both speak of work, family, but he tells her things she already knows, like he is afraid she has forgotten him, like these thoughts are frostbitten corpses she has left behind.

In her sketch there are no streets, only neurons. There are no harbors, only hands. Everything spirals out like a fingerprint.

I don't want to tell you what to do, he offers in the quiet.

She blinks. It's two in the morning, she croaks. The world is made of meandering lines.

How about something less abstract.

That doesn't sound like a question.

Don't get emotional. It's just a thought.

I'm not emotional.

She flaps open her sketchpad, parchment roughing against fingerpads. In her mind a spatter of oil and waves and churning ice. He is always present in her maps now, they all are, cliffs like her father's words and oceans of her mother's silence and of course him, always slightly caustic, always burning away routes that lead elsewhere.

Please, he says. I just want it to be good.

This time she sketches boundless continents untethered by one another, by anything terrestrial. The cartographer walks away as the tundra and oceans and plains bleed across the startled wideness of the page and the mapmaker lets him go, continues to fill these expanses with butterflied tracks and blooming expeditions and spiraling journeys because she knows the depths and breadths of the world are no longer empty, can never be empty again.

3

Survival in the Plague Years

Bubonic Plague

We imagine serpents of pestilence thrashing in their flesh, caressing with fang tips. It burns in bodies we no longer touch, fearing their breath, their handprints, will scald us. The hearth fire illuminates our wives' once proud eyes, our children who used to tug our beards and clasp our dirty thumbs with their whole tiny hands.

We do not know how to make them comfortable, do not know how to tend to them. Their underarms heavy with evil-colored bloats, poisonous fruit. Lips cracked with dried blood. We lean close enough to press a shirt that smells like us, feels like us, to their fingers, then shy away.

We clutch vinegar-dipped rags to our mouths, our noses, and the whole world tastes of bitterness. Our sorrow chased away by guilt. Guilt for the stares at our boarded windows, cracks of light arrowing through. Guilt for our moments of wild panic, when we pitch ourselves against the door, scream for help, help, we are dying.

But the watchmen shout that we are cowards.

We carry our families in our clothes, our lungs, as the alcohol-thick scent of disintegration, terror. Sew their image into our swollen eyelids, the way they grope for us, all blackened sores and gasps.

We already think of them as memories. Choke on the ashes of how they were—our children with skin like fresh-laid eggs, our wives with blown-glass bodies. How they taste now—as dark empty spaces where we huddle, watching as they perish.

Cholera

At the harbor we search for our husbands. See only their ship, dipping and arching, anchor chain taut.

The sky froths with storm clouds. Waves slam on the dock.

We ask the doctors, who ebb and flow along the greasy planks: Why do they not come ashore?

Their words are ironclad: We cannot allow it.

Our thoughts maelstroms, pitching, yawing. We have not seen our men in years. Imagine them with thick stiff beards, rimed with sea salt, smelling of wind. We have not heard anything of their lives, where they have been, who they have lost, why they were gone at all, and what it is they could not find with us.

We ask why we cannot see them, cannot go aboard.

They wave us off. Say the disease, it will kill us all. Their spectacles awash with dying light.

Let us go to them, we beg. Perhaps they can be healed.

We receive no reply.

Waves leap. Purple-black clouds loom, a bruise. We see no one abovedecks, no signals, no one shouting. The air thick, a wake spinning after the blame that cuts through us, the anger.

It must be something they gave themselves, we say, smoothing our hair. Something that hunted them over the waves, over the islands they visited. The women they knew.

We gather along the harbor breakfront, the stone flattened and smoothed by waves. As raindrops pelt us, sea spray sinks into our skin, cracked from washing. Scouring. Cooking. We imagine our husbands curled in their bunks, sinewy bundles waiting for a first cough, first sniff, first stomach turn. We want to tend them, heal them.

We climb the wall. Cast off our skirts, our shoes, our corsets. Unpin our hair.

Shouts behind us.

Their echoes are waves. Lapping at our empty hulls.

Yellow Fever

With nods to one another across the dim tent, we begin the experiment.

Hypothesis, that mosquitoes carry the disease, not miasma.

The subjects ourselves, white men and one woman.

The procedure, to cup infected insects to our slippery-veined arms. Perfect specimens all.

We are silent, except for breaths. Short and harsh in the humidity.

The mosquitoes dip and swim in their jars. Closer, closer. They land and we think this is it, but the quickening of our own pulses disturbs them.

New cases breed, day by day. Too many to count. Our log books full, time and date and treatment and burial plot. The soldiers we have seen wounded in battle, nurses who swept across the field without fear. All at once they fall to a disease with no cure. Chill, fever, heaving breath and jaundiced skin. Their eyes with hints of yellow, like the edges of old photographs.

In our bodies, we decided, we can find a cure. It is the only way.

We will not write to our families.

While the dying thrash and sweat and ache, we still ourselves, our breathing, our minds. We wait for the prick that will allow us to stop their suffering.

Count the seconds to lower our heartbeats. Count the wingtaps against our skin. Count the time before we too will burn.

Leprosy

When the men come, all precision, they do not knock. Tear through our homes with lightning quickness, rip our children from their beds.

We their mothers do not try to shield their cricked hands, which bend like roots, their weeping-eye sores.

Our voices like leaves brushing against skin, we ask, where do you take them?

We stay back, do not fight. Have wondered in the dark, since our children took ill, whether we should try and keep them. Whether it is best.

Our husbands strike, eruptions and flame.

We reach for them, as driftwood reaches for shore. Soft. Weak.

When our children weep, call to us, these small versions of ourselves our husbands asked for, we are shocked by the small ways we miss them. Because we wondered, hearing of the colony, if we would all be better off. Now they beat against us in sandfleck moments, moments that leave bite marks along our necks.

Our children are placed in carts, leave us, rattle away somewhere we cannot follow.

We throw open the door, wanting to chase them, throw ourselves into their bodies. But sunlight collects on our skin. The air is fresh, clean. It is different from our homes, with them and without them. Shouts, laughter, scents of bread and lush flowers. Trees hang over us, leaves green and dripping dew. Everything is sweet, tastes of life before our children, before our husbands, before we were tethered to anyone except the Earth and its movements, when its upheavals were the only violence we knew. When its quakes were the only faults we felt through our marrow. For a moment we forget our husbands and their shouts, their pounding against the walls. Forget the disarray of our children.

We forget what we wanted to tell them, until they have faded into distance. Forget that we wanted to tell them the world is emptier, now that they are gone, and we are emptier too.

Typhus

We ignite funeral pyres, we who are walking corpses ourselves.

Outside the walls our enemies mass, make themselves known in tents and battering rams and tiny specks of light.

They watch. Wait for the fires to die, for the moment to strike.

Days and days bring no relief. The air ripples with flame. We, sweat draining from our pores, hands tingling with soot and burns, miss the roars of others, of those who yearn to destroy us. We miss enemies who need us, our city, so they can feel like conquerors. We miss enemies whose hatred is a poison we feel in the tips of arrows.

They move no closer.

Weeks pass and more of us fall ill. We sleep in the streets. Tend the fires.

The armies march away. They leave their campfires as withered embers, their hopes of conquering in tent pegs and hoof prints.

They look back, meet our wasted eyes.

We watch our foes trickle on, blood from a wound. We thought they would stay, thought they would watch us, attack us, do anything but leave.

We wipe our scorched-hair arms across our faces, only smudge ourselves further. Our bellies rumble, hollow. Our hair long and unkempt, wallowing in sweat and grit. Our homes cobwebbed and dusty with ash, the only thing we have produced in weeks.

We throw down our pikes, our swords, the ones we have used to tend the flames. We cast off our masks of damp cloth that were once uniforms.

We leave the bodies burning. Stumble past the walls, the gates. Chase the ones who would harm us, who pitied us, who left us.

Invade us, we beg, as they shake us off, dust away our cremated handprints.

We ask them to prove we are still wanted, needed. Prove we mean everything. Prove our destruction will matter at all.

HIV

They tell us, the priests and other men with demon grins and brimstone eyes, that if we lie with an untouched pure woman, we will be cured.

We will pray to find them, we say. We will pray.

We find our wives at home, children on their hips or at their breasts. They speak little, ask where we have been. We feel there is a hardness, a bitterness in their words, in their voices, that sharpens, as though we are whetstones. As though we hone them. As though, without us, they will be blunted, dull. They do not say this, but we believe we know.

We watch in muddy streets, swirling with steam after rain, spy girls too young for short dresses, quicksilver smiles like full chalices and warm tawny eyes. We take their fleshy arms, bid them come with us. When we feel them shiver we pretend their fear is nothing compared to ours, which peppers our vision with flecks of emptiness, vast swathes of our lives where divine light does not reach.

We do not look into their faces smeared with tears. Pretend their cries are hallelujahs, that they rejoice in our sanctification.

With our hands carving bruises deep under their skin, our hips wet, we are nothing but fear, nothing but thoughts of how death comes slowly, how death will waste us away.

We thrust and thrust and thrust, recite the gospels of our fears, until we cannot anymore. We wipe ourselves, slick and warm, tell ourselves we are not the same, we are transformed. And this, at least, is true. We are bodies that should be exhausted but infect, vessels that should be holy but are not.

4

The Lemurians

We were ten and eleven when my younger brother fell in love with his only friend, a boy named Marcus. They became obsessed with Lemuria, the mythical lost continent of the Pacific, and I listened to them on Saturday afternoons, creating their own version of this paradise. My brother swoony, mapping its cities, its volcanoes and jungles, sketching its people and beaches and marble sculptures.

That autumn my brother drew a picture for Marcus, one he'd revised for weeks: two boys holding hands, one human, one made of sand. I couldn't tell which was meant to be Marcus and which was my brother, but their grips were equally tender, equally fierce. The sand boy's fingertips crinkled backward, sloughing away, pressing crimped divots into the flesh of the other boy, salting his skin with grit.

I tried to convince him to keep it, tried to protect him. Marcus may not feel the same, I told him. I'm your older sister. Trust me.

But my brother, softened and unspooling and hopeful, said, he'll like it.

I watched from the hall as he gave the picture to Marcus, the two of them in our kitchen.

Eww, Marcus said. He stared at my brother like he was a spider, some creature that had no right to be near him.

The paper fluttered to the ground.

I could feel my brother's silence, the deep vacuum of his need, like I did when he sat alone or when someone asked him how he was and for several breaths he couldn't decide how to answer.

I pounced from behind the door frame. Pick it up.

Marcus didn't move.

My brother's eyes ponded with tears.

I shoved Marcus. Pick it up.

Why?

I pushed him again, hard. He flopped to the ground, the page crushed under him.

You're both crazy, shouted Marcus. He screamed over his shoulder as he leapt up, ran from the house. You freaks.

My brother was not allowed to play with Marcus anymore. I was grounded.

The drawing was left on the floor of the kitchen, the Lemurian boys holding one another for dear life, crumpled at the middle. I returned for it later, intending to rip it apart and maybe throw it in Marcus's face at school. But it was something my brother created, something cherished by him, and as I moved to shred the two boys, I stopped. They were so fragile, these hopes of my brother's, these dreams of mythical places, and I couldn't bear to destroy even this sheet of paper.

He cried in his room that night. I snuck out after hiding the drawing in my bookcase and sat with him. Still he sketched the Lemurians, the land he imagined so perfectly. I tried to make him feel better by asking questions: What do they build out of? What games do they play? What do Lemurians look like?

He answered with rooftops slanted like waves, with children throwing balls of kelp, with people sculpting others out of sand.

I asked him, why Lemuria?

He told me the story of his lost continent, the world he imagined. As he did so, he drew the boys again, hand in hand. One made of flesh, one made of beach.

It is customary for the people of Lemuria to sculpt the ones they love. For the humans to create mates from beach detritus—shells, sand, sea glass. To craft hair from kelp and find wave-polished stones for eyes just the right shade of abyss black or deepened blue or storm grey.

The process takes weeks, even months, for the Lemurians build their lovers without tools, without molds. They take great care so they do not have to start again.

When at last the seashell people come to life, they shudder like beings emerging from water, as though they do not understand the skin they are in. They smell of wet earth and sea breeze and great stale depths. They scan the sky, the Earth, their creators. When they unfold their fish scale–tipped fingers and stretch their hands, it is the Lemurians they reach for.

They ask, who are we?

The Lemurians respond, ours.

My school years were punctured by absence, by suspensions, by the battles of my brother fought by me. He stood to the side, helpless, his sand dune face perpetually shifting, collapsing.

I was suspended for punching a boy who called my brother a fag in sixth grade, in seventh grade, in eighth grade. I waited until the last second to intervene, poised beside my wide-eyed sibling. Each time I hoped he would fight for himself.

Only boys hit each other, my father told me every time I was punished.

But he wasn't going to do it, I explained. He needs me.

My brother drew me as a Lemurian, a warrior queen. He slipped the page under my door. My hands were made of sea glass, tinted red.

The seashell people are everything the Lemurians want. They are demure, or witty, or stoic, or meek, whatever characteristics their creators desire. They move like ribbons of silt trapped in currents and their voices are sounds magnified in conch shells, swelled and echoing. When they walk they make a soft grating sound and sometimes small chunks of hardened sand sift to the ground in their wake.

The seashell people are tall and strong and can walk for miles without tiring, but, like humans, they are imperfect. The Lemurians must keep them away from water, hold them inside when it rains, avoiding the grass on dewy mornings, never stray past the tide line on the beach, for the water would erode their creations on contact.

The seashell people grow restless, shifty, especially during storms.

What does it feel like, they ask their creators, tracing the tendrils of raindrops down windows, following each slither and writhe.

Water? It feels like nothing.

But we want to know, they say. We want to feel it too.

It feels like pain, the Lemurians lie. It feels like extinction, rippling over your skin.

They are for protection, the untruths. The Lemurians believe this at their core, though they cannot be sure if the protection is for the seashell people alone or for themselves as well, for the pulsing beating emptiness always there, dormant and waiting.

My brother emerged from middle school as a soccer star. He found a girlfriend, several more girlfriends. Sometimes they came over and would tease my brother about his handwriting or the way he spoke with a barely-real lisp. I always wondered if they knew, if they had some inkling they were trying to name. I jumped in without being asked, defended him, but it was always my brother who laughed it off, who said, it's just a joke. He projected a charm that bordered on arrogance.

He hid the Lemurians in a portfolio under his bed.

I wondered if I was the only one who saw his eyes on his friend Vince during soccer warm-ups, tracing the power of his legs, his boxy jaw, his chest with sprigs of hair.

The Lemurians enjoy years of plenty. They walk the grand boulevards of their cities. They sit atop the hills surrounding the ocean, noticing how the seashell people lean forward, how they watch the waves all crowned with foam.

Sometimes the Lemurians awaken to find the seashell people in doorways, staring into the night. They explain that they are watching dew collect in the mouths of leaves and flowers, or eyeing the condensation that frosts the walls.

The Lemurians lock their homes at night for fear their creations will slip away, that they will wake up and find only puddles of watery sand, only shells and kelp strands and two handpicked stones in a clump.

High school passed this way: my brother excelling on the soccer field, spending evenings drawing and weekends with Vince, no longer needing a defender, leaving me fighting just to fight, leaving me with my atrophying aggression. Like the Lemurian queen, I became a warrior with no continent to protect.

So the summer before my senior year was all want. The boys clumsy and quick—cocks removed from rainbows of boxers, legs shaking with effort, foreplay in backseats, maneuvering for space like circling armies.

Vince was always at our house, close enough to touch. He was sharp, athletic; he flirted with the energy of a late bloomer, a boy discovering what it was to be young and beautiful. But my brother knew this and collapsed the space around them, especially when I was in the room—always talking, always moving between us. That summer was my brother's want, too—hanging in the air like decaying fruit, like apples rotting on the tree.

Whenever he was away from Vince, my brother crafted alternate worlds where cliffs became crooks of knees and elbows, features became caves and alpine vistas. Every drawing, every painting of Lemuria was a rendering of him, a map of his emotions, his palm tree body. There was yearning in every canvas, yearning only I could see; every paintbrush or pen or marker he held bled with it, seemed to leach pent-up sadness from him. Like blood, there was always more.

The seashell people became lovelier. The scoops of their shoulders, the coronas of their heads. The jutting of their spiny cheeks, the rippling hardness of their eyes.

The cataclysms start gradually, with tremors and rockslides, and the Lemurians barely notice. They walk with the seashell people, they shop in the markets, they hike into the hills lush with vegetation.

It is not until the storms begin, bringing floods and mudslides, that the Lemurians worry. The seashell people beg to be let outside, even as the volcanoes erupt, even as the sky becomes a dilated pupil, focused and black.

The seashell people ask their creators for explanations, but the Lemurians have none, except that the world is ending.

We must escape, say the seashell people, walking past their creators. We must leave.

We do not know how.

But the seashell people are already snaking off their lovers' arms, throwing open the doors. They are already marching through the smoke, through the thunder.

My brother had never had sex, never had boasts about weekends or parties. His teammates could smell it on him, the otherness creeping at his shoulder. I was afraid for him, afraid enough that I began spreading rumors, hoping to create a reputation from thin air: how my brother was out all night with a senior from Catholic, how my brother had never loved anyone, how he was a different person than everyone thought, how my brother was not spending his teenage years drawing unreal places he could never go.

His girlfriend dumped him when she heard the stories, confronted him over the phone in front of Vince and me sitting in our living room. He turned on me afterward, rage hanging thick and tight about him, an ill-fitting ugly coat. He'd never been this angry before, never at me, and he cornered me on the couch.

You nosy bitch, he exploded.

Hey. Vince tried to usher him away. You were just saying you might dump her.

That's not the goddamn point.

Don't worry about it.

Don't protect her, my brother said, full of venom.

What do you know about protecting? I pushed him away from me, connecting with his gut. He stumbled back.

You bitch, my brother hissed. I don't need you. No one fucking needs you.

He cradled his hands in front of him, collapsed over his waist. Trying to keep something from spilling, something in that moment I wanted to tear out, to gouge away, something I wanted to leave shattered on the ground.

The Lemurians follow the seashell people to the beach, lightning crackling above, begging them to stop, snatching at their arms, their hands.

We want to escape, the seashell people say. They are digging their toes into the sand. They are listening to the waves, one long procession, smashing.

You cannot leave us, say the Lemurians.

We are only human.

The seashell people are turning to the gray-blue sea, the air all spray and brine. Each dart of water disintegrates them a miniscule amount.

You are ours, beg the Lemurians, who fear they will be left alone, fear the unforming of who they are.

And before the Lemurians know what they are doing, they are destroying the seashell people. While the ground crumbles and the ash falls and the darkness creeps, the Lemurians smash what they have loved.

Vince left after my brother retreated to his room that night. I walked him to the door, still shaking, and he squeezed my arms, searched my face, asked if I was all right. It was genuine, no trace of mocking in his voice, no sliver of teasing in his lamplit face.

I understood why my brother loved him then, understood that all his energy concealed oceans of kindness. I understood it all and was still desperately angry, angry at my weak little brother and at myself and maybe even at Vince, maybe just a bit.

I kissed him as an answer, his hands in my hair, under my shirt; we had sex in his car, until I was only pulse and dark and whatever cataclysm destroyed Lemuria. Which was all I could think about, with him inside me: the extinctions of that continent, silent and lost forever.

The air is thick around the Lemurians, superheated and spinning. They cradle the remains of their seashell lovers like children, like tiny beings they can bear into existence.

They are trying to click the pieces back together, trying to recall how they did it the first time. Maybe they can fix it all—the apocalypses, every one, the destructions large and small—but everything is swirling, everything is hazy with ash and soot. It stains their hands and their faces, makes rivers stand out on their skin. It blankets everything, even the shells, even the sand.

My brother knew, of course he knew. Vince told me this, took my hands and told me that my brother didn't care.

What did he look like, I asked.

What do you mean? Vince moved to kiss me. I don't know. He looked like himself.

But I knew—that collapsing sand face, that empty tide half-smile. I imagined him seeing Vince's car down the street, seeing it still there and checking and checking and had he drawn the Lemurians then, their annihilations, their very ends?

I tried once to talk to my brother about it. I went to his room not long after, knocked and knocked. He shouted from his desk for me to come in, not turning around. He asked if dinner was ready; he was drawing, he said, and wouldn't be down until later.

No, I said. I stood behind him, saw how he maneuvered to hide his work. I caught a slash of seaweed hair, billowing past his elbow, a fragment of wave and glistening smoke.

Can I see? I nodded toward his paper.

He snorted. I'm not sure you'd get it.

I always have.

I reached for the page. He blocked me, shifted his whole weight in front of my hand. No, he said, voice booming.

We stayed this way, our breath following one another's, so the room was never silent.

Why can't you draw something real instead of this delusional shit, I asked him, heat consuming my gut, my chest, my face. Why can't you draw things that actually exist?

He shifted, revealing bits of seashell scattered across sand.

Maybe they were real, once. Maybe now they're just not places you can actually go.

He stared at me for one long beat, finally turning back to his desk.

Behind the debris, behind the Lemurians, was a sky melting, was a land crumbling.

In the end, Lemuria is simply gone. The humans, their seashell lovers, their houses facing the sunrise.

We dipped in and out of touch after I graduated and started at university. He went to art school a year later. We spent flustered, frantic holiday visits drinking too much and forming a coalition against our parents. But we always left rigid, taut, like limbs needing and unable to stretch after an awkward sleep.

I took the Lemurian queen with me. My brother saw me from the hall and said, Jesus Christ, throw that shit away.

I didn't know how to tell him: the drawing was the most complete picture of me, the most complete I had ever felt.

My brother's first art installation after he graduated college was called Lemuria. I RSVP'd yes on the Facebook event page, one of hundreds of invitees. The gallery's website advertised my brother as one of the up-and-coming young talents and called his work a convergence of raw emotion and deft style.

I went alone to the gallery, a gin and tonic greasy in my stomach. It was a trendy place, all clear straight lines and brightness, full of women who moved like mermaids, graceful and thin, men with artfully disheveled hair. As soon as I arrived I could see this version of Lemuria was different from the one I'd known in childhood: there was no love, no hope in these Lemurians, no longing in their seashell creations. They were monstrous, murky and shadowed, hemorrhaging sand.

I found him chatting with his boyfriend near the front of the gallery, a midsized place already bustling. The gin churned in my stomach.

Of course, I remarked. We hugged, our stiffness like a reef, a barrier.

Of course what?

His words a hook, dangling in open water.

I always wondered when the lost continent would resurface.

Oh, he laughed. He took a plastic cup of white wine from his partner, whose arm grazed his elbow. I'm pretty happy with how they turned out.

He sipped.

They're different, I remarked. But the alcohol could not make the words light, breezy.

Those were so stupid. Kid stuff, you know?

I searched the walls. Behind my brother hung a painting of what looked like the entire continent of Lemuria swallowed by flame.

I still have the one you gave me. The warrior.

Jesus. He laughed, a spear of a sound. I hoped you would've destroyed it.

The hubbub seemed to increase, background sounds like the crashing of waves. I almost told him I kept it in my desk under a stack of bills. I almost told him I thought about them, the Lemurians, anytime it rained, anytime it stormed, anytime it felt like the world was washing away.

Well, he continued. Have a look around. I should mingle.

Oh. Sure.

He was absorbed into a group of friends as soon as I replied, leaning into his boyfriend's side and laughing. He didn't look back.

I grabbed a cup of red wine, watched the scarlet as it prismed across my fingers in the brightness. I traveled alone through my brother's artwork, roaming swathes of emptiness, jumbles of shells, faces disintegrating into sand. Gone were the maps of those he loved, the blank slate skies, the sharpened mountaintops. Instead I found disappearing shores, vanishing cities, fading mirages from which no one escaped.

I paused at a charcoal drawing awash with blacks and grays. On it tangled two beings, violent and contorting, mouths chasmed open, stalked by a dark wave. Collapsing, rupturing, snarled together, a knot of sand and wreckage and rage, an extinguishing I could feel in my gut. It was all cataclysm, this Lemuria surrounding me. It was all annihilation. It was all the last moment, all looming destruction, all fracturing seashell bodies.

5

Extinction Events Proposed by My Father

1. The dinosaurs gas themselves to death. The emissions of hundred-ton creatures create a planet heavy and toxic.

My father, a man who ran out his life with searching for the cause of the dinosaurs' annihilation, proposed this theory around the time of my birth: that the dinosaurs, through their very existence, their bodily functions, eliminated themselves. It was the first of many such theories for which he became known, and it followed me my entire life.

I read his *Journal of Paleontology* article repeatedly in my childhood, wanting to understand extinctions as I then thought he did. He kept it in his study his whole life, until throwing it out upon my discovery of the Chicxulub crater many years later. He would pull it out often, his first publication, the start of something that ached and ached his whole life. I took it with me as he shuffled me to my grandparents' home, snuggled in my bag against the stuffed mammoths I was told my mother had given me at birth; my father would look on them with a mixture of disgust and longing, muttering something about survival.

I wondered if he knew how the thick pages got to be crinkled, torn, or if he assumed it was from his own rereading.

My grandparents discovered me night after night, tracing the words, memorizing them under a flashlight. In these moments, caverned under the sheets, I imagined myself under the Earth, excavating the answers my father searched for.

I never told him. I think, perhaps, he might have been surprised.

2. The dinosaurs suffer from a diminution of sexual activity and find themselves with no desire to procreate or parent their already existing offspring.

My father left me with my maternal grandparents for much of my childhood, people who existed behind a veil of decrepitude, when he traveled on digs in foreign countries. They were Catholic and would go to Mass every Sunday. I slipped into the confessional and said nothing, only, forgive me, Father, I do not want to be here.

I only wished to worship with my own father, who prayed to the Earth, desperate and thinning, his theories becoming prayers. The hacking of his pick and the swish of his brush and the sifting of sediment, catechisms.

I desired, rather than let the decay of age doom my world, to excavate it. Loop it through my fingers like the rosaries my grandparents held every night when they forced me to kneel and ask forgiveness. Forgiveness, they told me, for the lack of faith I showed in yearning to follow my father's path.

You and your mother, they said, palming her photograph as though running their fingers through her hair, whisking their voices over her memory as though they could feel her still. You and your mother, faithless. We told her, too, that you will only find answers in God. You will not find answers in the Earth.

I did not understand how they could perceive me as faithless; I had faith, though I could not yet articulate its manner. Faith in destructions, faith in endings, faith in searching for preserved breaths of the dead.

I never spoke to my father about this when he was home; he

inhabited his study like the remains of some creature left behind by flood or eruption, covered by layers of decay. I pretended to relish the silence, reading through his bookshelves, mimicking him as he sat behind his desk or on the couch, hands folded over his forehead, lips never moving.

I asked him questions and questions. Rather than tell me to stop reading and go play in the yard, he gave exhausted answers, ones I could not interpret or define, that emptied themselves into the air, reluctant.

What is the Permian, I asked. So general, at first. What is a sediment?

Then, as my interest increased, my questions narrowed, and his voice landed somewhere between frustration and amusement.

What did the dinosaurs sound like when they breathed? How long does an extinction take?

He replied: The breaths of dinosaurs sounded like echoes off the wall of a cave.

Some say an extinction takes all of time.

3. *The dinosaurs are victims of widespread mammalian conspiracies involving the eating of eggs and other resources necessary for survival.*

My father returned periodically, and the house eroded with each word we spoke, collected ice cracks each time I asked about my mother, wind and water when I asked to join him on his next trip to India or Australia or Ethiopia.

She had ghosts of cheekbones, my father told me once. The skin stretched so thin it was as though it was never there. Her lips, rims of craters. She created stark boundaries—before and after meeting her—in people because she was like implosions and destructions in her bones, in her voice.

He would tell me these things, sometimes without my asking. As though he could ascribe some shape of her to my own. He told me once how she did not sing to me in the womb, but read her work to me as she would write.

He said, I always knew when she was happy with the work she'd done in a day, when it was good, because I came home and she'd say she felt you kick at this phrase, at this word, at this idea. I asked to read it, to hear it, too, but she always laughed, and she would tell me that her daughter was already a much better critic than I.

It was after this conversation that my father agreed to take me with him, on the condition that I learn more than I could from books.

When he told my grandparents, they said he was crazy to do this. A girl needs stability, they said. How young she is, how like her parents.

But he laughed, his guffaw like the Earth's hollowness after eruptions, told them how foolish they were, that his daughter was almost thirteen.

She's ten, they argued.

He registered no surprise, except to say, well thank goodness. Her lack of publications will be acceptable.

This was the only joke I ever heard my father make.

4. The dinosaurs suffer from racial senility. Reaching an evolutionary dead end, their genetic novelty desiccates and their species becomes old and decrepit and inadaptable.

My father had a partner on his digs. A woman, with whom I shared a tent. She was the only woman on any expedition. Her hands were as rough as the men's, but they arrowed over rock with a poise, a knowledge I wondered if my mother had possessed. I watched her for hours and she let me assist her in removing fossils, bones, from the ground, an honor my father never accorded me. Her voice gentled around me. She had no daughters, she told me, only boys, children around my age whose only interests were sports.

She told me once: your father will try to tell you there are only two stages, before and after. He will try to tell you nothing survives an extinction event, that nothing bleeds through, that there is no such thing as backward or forward contamination, the spilling over of creatures after an extinction, into other eras. He believes these things to be extreme and quick and finished in a blaze. He does not think these things drain one another; he only believes in emptiness on one end and fullness on the other. Never a mixture.

I remembered how I had read his publications, his numerous articles on the demise of the dinosaurs across years, how he had told me that we are the products of two stages, always speaking of my mother. Before. After. A peak and a void.

She sighed, her brush delicately hovering over a crinoid in the cliff face. Look, she told me. If we are above the boundary, as we are, this should not be here. It is a creature that existed at the time of the extinction, so what business has it here, unless the boundary weaves? Unless the dying out of species does not happen all at once?

Across the grains of sediment purled lines, etchings of debris.

She said: your father scoffs when I point this out, every time. When I show him, yes, it does exist, it has trickled over the boundary, he will move onto another segment where the line is more obvious, fits his theory better.

That makes no sense, I told her. How many times had I read that the nature of science is discovery and reevaluation?

No. She scraped away the clay, the scree, from the fossil. It swirled in her palm, curved shell wrapping the air around itself. Because you understand—there is only unbearable decline.

5. The dinosaurs are poisoned by uranium absorbed from the soil.

My father sent me to get my doctorate. I chose my mother's alma mater and wondered if the common air, the common surfaces we had touched or the pavement we had walked somehow seeped the two of us together.

My name was familiar to my professors and classmates; the teachers looked at me with an air of sadness, accused me of plagiarism in the first weeks of the semester when my research proved more accurate than they assumed, less insane than they might have hoped.

My classmates never warmed to me fully. They asked at first whether I was helping my father with his latest venture, how my research on the gassing of the dinosaurs was going, whether I had found an answer for the Permian extinction involving extraterrestrials. And I laughed, then worked through the night. My apartment was a litter of books and papers; any men who came in gave up walking across the bedroom, the kitchen, and, eventually, the living room, leaving themselves only the space at the threshold of the door in which to contain their affection.

My father called sporadically, his voice stretching across the days and weeks like continental drift, moving toward something unknown and unobtainable. He asked what I was studying and in the background I heard South Africa, China.

When I told him what I searched for, how I was sure an asteroid had killed the dinosaurs, he laughed, a cavern of a laugh, and said, may your luck be stronger than mine.

6. The dinosaurs are destroyed by particles from a faraway supernova.

My father called me from home the day I earned my doctorate. I had not expected him to be in the country. It soon became clear he was intoxicated, and I asked him, softly, as I would have scraped away the dust from a bone, why wasn't he in the Rift Valley?

Sick, he said.

With what?

A long time I've been sick.

He said no more than this, wanting me to pry and dig and cajole, but I heard the sound of my classmates on the stairs outside my apartment and had already had some whiskey. There was a silence that came gaping over us, spawning other malignant graved silences.

I'm a doctor now, I said. This morning.

I heard his teeth scrape along the mouth of a bottle before he said, and you feel more intelligent now? Qualified to determine the illnesses of the Earth?

The footsteps of my classmates were leaking away. Yes, I replied.

Because I did not want to know whether his answer would have been different, I hung up.

7. The dinosaurs are obliterated by entropy. As the universe slopes into chaos, so do their atoms.

My father called with the increasing frequency of earthquakes before a volcanic eruption, after he told me he was ill. He chased me with his voice across the world, his voice that lost boom with the days, crumbling under its own weight. I searched for what had eluded him.

He told me of the research he was still doing, book dust in his lungs, joints creaking when he shifted. He asked where I was but never what I had found.

I told him, I'm getting closer. We've found a gravitational anomaly in the Yucatan. Some shocked quartz.

He said, it couldn't possibly be an impact that killed them. You won't find anything.

He didn't answer when I told him otherwise, that the underwater arc at Chicxulub looked like an eye, too perfectly rounded to be accidental; instead he told me about my childhood, my mother.

The first thing I published was when I met your mother, he said. I wrote this article when I was waiting in the hospital for you to be born. And on and on. Trying to construct around me a tomb of sediment in which to encase the version of myself, which was more like my mother, which was the one he chose to remember, to preserve, to fossilize.

8. The dinosaurs are destroyed by a cataclysm, a cryptoexplosion, which leaves the Earth nearly barren. It is this that kills the dinosaurs and not an asteroid impact, despite findings and evidence to the contrary.

My father did not listen, choked and scoffed, when I told him over the phone of my discovery.

The murderous crater was there, palmed into the coast of the Yucatan. Leveled on my radars, the Earth tendered over it in folds, cenotes freckled along its edge. We analyzed sample after sample, determined this could only be the result of a massive impact, a decimating blow. My first thought was of my father, how he would wither when I told him, how I had memorized his words so long ago and how it was all for this. How his research would level into plains, into alluvium, into deltas where erosion scattered them.

My father left me nothing in the moment I called him to tell him of this, nothing but the clogged taste of soil, the feeling of chasing. He whispered, you found it?

I let the silence corrode.

I don't believe it. It couldn't be that. His voice drifting.

I heard the rustling of papers, the scattering of ideas in a growing void.

I felt the eras and epochs of his life shattered then, against the hollowed crater walls, against the dust and erosions of the Earth. They tasted of unfamiliar words, ones wombed in a woman I had never met.

9. It does not matter how the dinosaurs are destroyed, only that they are, only that they perish, only that their existence never mattered.

We spoke once after my discovery. He said, we met on a dig.

I was typing, so my response was narrowed between the fault lines of keystrokes. I replied, I need to finish this paper.

He whispered, your mother found fish bones in the extinction line of the boundary we were investigating. I told her, it must be a mistake. There's no way it wasn't killed at the outset. There's no way anything could survive a sudden demolition like this.

I waited for him to tell me something new.

She said, your mother: life will linger. It will leach everything.

He hung up shortly after.

I believed my father left me nothing upon my discovery of the crater, but this has never been true. He left a span of time, memories scattered in erratics, splicing the heart of such an era into uneven plots, pocked with grooves and silt and his periods of absence, which manifested even in the spaces between his words, his pickstroke smile, his glaciated voice. He left me a knowledge, degrading until there was no before, no after, only fragments and fossils of the way things were once, the way they might have been.

6

The Disaster Preparedness Guidebook

The earthquake strikes on the morning Brooke starts her new job. She is lying awake when the bed swoons, the lamps rattle, empty moving boxes leap from the dresser. It is her first earthquake and she is breathless, adrenaline-washed, because for a moment the ground is liquefied and she wishes she could slip through, could be absorbed by the convulsing planet.

When it is over the few photos on the wall are askew. Brooke's husband is clenching her arm, his whole body curled toward hers, a survivor clutching a raft.

You okay?

Crazy, he stutters. He exhales and releases her but does not relax.

For a second the corners of his eyes crinkle and he is about to smile and the vague, tense edges against which Brooke has been cutting herself are smoothed. She shivers, then laughs, and her whole body feels loose and flexible and dangerous. Tendrils of excitement seep into her like fingers, finding spaces and filling them. She stands, pulls on her robe.

Why don't you get up with me?

But he shakes his head, swaddles himself in blankets.

Brooke brews herself a cup of tea—the electric kettle was one of the first things she unpacked—and sips it from the deck of their new home. Sunlight licks its way up the volcano looming to the west, a golden tongue over a vast craggy tooth. At a height of nearly ten thousand feet, the peak appears closer than it is, the most domineering in the mountain range stretching north and south of the midsized town to which they've just moved, the most prominent vertebrae in the spine of a dormant, eternally buried creature.

The morning is clear, dew specking the wood beneath Brooke's feet, and demarcations are visible on the slope, deciduous woods becoming coniferous, coniferous bleeding out into stone, into the smooth, bald peak. Stray wisps of cloud hover just above the line between coniferous forest and rock, and a procession of lights can barely be made out, snaking along the road to the summit, the only signs of people who have made the climb to watch the sunrise. Below them the lights of the town glitter, scatter out from the base, dazzle like snowflakes that have not yet melted. Brooke positions her mug so the steam spirals with the steam from the summit, two gray trails blending into the open-wound sky.

The history of the volcano—her volcano, Brooke already thinks of it—is comprised of extinction. Scientists found ash from its first prehistoric eruption in ice core samples; it was later responsible for the annihilation of an entire Native American tribe, then a pioneer settlement centuries later. Residents still unearth pots and hatchets while planting potatoes, find tools and bones in their yards after heavy rains. Construction on all new homes was recently banned when a contractor found human remains while digging a foundation.

Brooke's husband saw the news story about the bones and printed off descriptions of other jobs for her, left them on her laptop with a bright orange sticky note. There was a smiley face, but something about the mouth reminded her of lacerations.

When she returns to the bedroom her husband is awake, laptop perched on the summit of his knees. He says, I've finished writing the first entry.

Of?

The disaster preparedness guidebook.

He is a field after a flood, vacant, washed away around the edges. He continues. The volcano's not extinct, you know.

When you mentioned it on the drive, I thought you were kidding.

His tone had been forced when he brought it up: what if, he'd said, what if I wrote something new?

Her husband is a technical writer, has never wanted to compose anything other than testing steps for new software, help pages, installation guides, so she'd laughed it off, grabbed a handful of chips from the bag on his lap, and promptly forgot.

He thrusts the laptop at her. *Do not stay inside if your house is damaged during the earthquake. Evacuate your home before you are buried.*

She sees him as she never has before, his body an uprooted tree, his hair a wave breaking backward, and she tells him, gentle, I was afraid of the earthquake too.

Her life with him has been full of tiny lies, falsehoods that build under her skin like follicles, because when she admits that the world does not frighten her the way it does him, he is clouded by insecurity.

She squeezes his hand. It's going to be fine.

I have to have a plan, just in case. We have to have a plan.

Brooke kisses his cheek, asks him to please unpack some boxes while she's at work.

His lips brace against air and he says, be careful.

Brooke's first marketing project for the national park is for Volcano Awareness Month, revising educational materials, classroom posters, brochures, producing material for Volcanothon, the park's outreach event. The park encompasses the volcano and the acres surrounding it, and she sinks into the vocabulary of disaster like a conversation with an old friend. Like she is a girl again, reading the same books on Mount St. Helens, Krakatoa, Vesuvius, on her volcano.

She enjoys driving to her office at the visitor center, halfway up the slope, nestled just below the twisting clouds, cruising the switchbacks like a finger up a spine, deftly, deliberately, the thick-growing woods loosening their hold with every foot. On the way home she pretends the world ends just beyond each curve of road and the volcano is all there is. She drives with her windows open, the air new and chilled, and she cannot help looking over her shoulder at the volcano, feeling its guardian-like presence always, even as she reaches the flat land at its base, as she passes through town, as she pulls into their garage.

One evening Brooke comes home after speaking in tolls and assessments all day, the terms for annihilations sticking to her lungs.

Progress, her husband says.

You got an interview?

Moving boxes are scattered throughout the living room, erratics left behind by some vast retreat, a slowly receding body.

He shakes his head, thrusts the laptop toward her. He has written several entries, but the only one she can grasp is the newest: Tornado.

If you are on the road during a tornado warning, seek shelter imme-diately. Under an overpass or in a ditch will do.

She is trying to think of something positive to say, something helpful, something comforting, in a voice that is not an avalanche, in words that do not drown out the sky with dust. Brooke grew up in tornado alley, southwest Missouri, where she learned to trace destruction in an ever-winding snake, sloughing its skin up from Texas, through Oklahoma City, through Tulsa, then through her.

Actually, you're not supposed to do this anymore.

That's what it says online.

They used to, but it turns out you can get sucked right out from an overpass.

You're the expert, he snaps.

She remembers it, the one true tornado, hazy in some places, sharp in others. Her mother's hands, speckled red and white. The faucet dripping over the roar until it was drowned out. Afterward it was half-gone, their house, and all that was left of her room was an empty backpack and her Earth Science textbook, sodden and warped.

Her husband shakes his head almost immediately, apologizes.

She had told him about the tornado on their second date, and he marveled at her like she had survived something monstrous, something terrible. She let him think this; it was easier than explaining the fascination, the gut-deep wonder that had been feeding off her fear until there was none left, until she was only wind, too, until she was all vacuum and pressure.

It's just stress, she tells her husband.

The next time he shows her a new entry he has changed nothing at all.

One Saturday Brooke's husband reads website after website. He starts several documentaries and finishes none of them.

It's too much, he says. How can you stand it, seeing them.

Onscreen, a pyroclastic flow barrels down a mountainside.

Brooke shakes his shoulder. We're going to the store.

If you could, would you make them stop?

It has never occurred to her, stopping the disasters. Even in her basement. Even when she emerged to see the kitchen mangled, the laundry room gone.

She shakes her head. Why would I?

I would, he says. I'd save everyone.

The last image, before she shuts off the TV, is Mount St. Helens before and after.

Brooke tells her mother about this interaction on the phone.

Change is hard for some men, sweetie. Try to get him out.

She had brought up the job slowly back in New York, wine glasses full. He did not believe her at first, incredulous that anyone could want to move, that anyone could hate it as she did.

I want something bigger, she said.

He cocked his head. Bigger than New York?

Every time she looked at the streets, the sky cut into slivers, she felt how small it was. The disasters from the volcano were extinctions, their massiveness stark, their devouring of communities, of people. They were real, they were ash clouds on the horizon, and when Brooke had read about them as a girl the words had vibrated with an expanding loss she wanted to understand, wanted for her own.

The following Monday the head of Volcanothon asks Brooke if she knows anyone who might volunteer for the event. We need someone to erupt the volcano at the end, the woman says, gesturing toward the front of the building, where a nearly ten-foot-tall scale model will sit to close out the event, erupting with bubbly goo.

Sure, Brooke says, my husband would be happy to help. Thinking of how he holds himself now, as though he carries some burden unknown to her. How he leaves the bills for her to pay in a collapsing pile, seeming all at once stung by their dwindling savings and his lack of contribution to them, before returning to the guidebook. How at their going-away party he had looked at her over the rim of his glass, like a distant moon over the curvature of the Earth. How his coworker assumed he was the one with the new job, did not even glance at Brooke when he asked, good money? And how her husband nodded, did not correct him. The small betrayals, soft and unique.

Brooke mentions to her husband that she has volunteered him for Volcanothon. We need the help, she tells him, plus it'll make me look good. And you might learn a few things about the volcano, you never know.

The crick in his neck like it is broken from inside.

A few days later a coworker invites Brooke to go hiking along the web of trails lining the lower elevations and base of the volcano. Have you seen the waterfall on the other side, she asks. It's no Yosemite Falls or anything, but it's still beautiful.

Brooke brings her husband and he wears running shoes and a thin windbreaker. She does not tell him he might be uncomfortable, chafing against the role of caretaker, under the weight of his suits hanging stiff with unuse, hair curling over his ears like a child.

Brooke's coworkers and their spouses with hardened-resin bodies dredge her husband with their eyes before setting off, Brooke flushing when one of them asks, do you hike much?

Her husband shakes his head and says, can you tell?

They are a small group, only six, but the conversation never ceases. Someone is always pointing out features of this particular boulder, the particular eruption that left it here, or where park rangers have located artifacts or ruins, or the oldest sections of the dense forest. Brooke absorbs it all, burns to know more, questions flowing from her; she wonders if she has ever felt so safe, ensconced and cradled in the underbellies of the rustling trees, the gurgling of streams, the volcano towering over them all. Without meaning to, she stops noticing her husband's labored breathing, his lingering footsteps.

About an hour in, they must cross a stream without a bridge. The group marches across, steady and sure and hopping on slick rocks.

Brooke's husband is the last to step forward, his weight soft on a wet stone everyone else has avoided.

Not that one, another one.

I've got it, he snaps.

The others are watching now, like creatures from the wild.

Come on, she urges him.

He mistakes the landing point and he stumbles and his full body weight pitches forward.

Then there is sputtering, and thrashing, and an uproar of laughter coming from Brooke too. She has not laughed this way in weeks. When he drags himself to the bank he is dripping and red.

I think I've hurt my ankle.

Jesus, you're fine.

Just give me the keys. I'll go back to the car.

There is a silence, a vicious clawmark of silence, the same kind of silence Brooke remembers sitting in her basement like a family member, knowing that in moments the world would shatter in a way that was not reparable, not completely.

Someone calls, everything all right?

Brooke turns and nods, a pinched motion.

You'll have more fun without me.

She recalls how her husband pointed out every storm cloud across the prairie, the shadowy bruises of volcanic detritus as they neared the Rockies. He shivered at the wide expanse of Theodore Roosevelt National Park, the grasslands swaying. Brooke swore he did not breathe as they crossed the Cascades, that he did not look anywhere but straight ahead.

She throws him the keys and follows her coworkers up the trail.

Brooke spends the rest of the hike vacillating between wild anger and deep guilt. They pass stone ruins and massive upturned trees and end at the waterfall on the other side of the volcano. Brooke snaps photographs and tries to send them to her husband, but they only bounce back. She watches her coworkers with their partners and feels a low-hanging fog of missing when she cannot even text him about the prism of the falls, the water droplets sparking her skin.

He apologizes when she climbs into the car.

She hands him the phone. You missed the waterfall.

He scrolls through her pictures.

How's your ankle?

His face is blank before he says, oh, fine.

While he was waiting, he tells her, he wrote another entry: *Flash floods are common during heavy rains. Be vigilant. You can be swept away easily, without notice.*

Brooke finds items lodged in her husband's jacket while doing laundry—a metrocard, a gift certificate to his favorite New York restaurant—and when she returns them he says, you know, for when we go back.

She calls her mother-in-law, asks if he's ever been this way before.

I don't know what to tell you, she replies. You moved him away from his comfort zone.

She begins editing his disaster plans, as if to fix something. These are things she knows, and she seeks to make his world a little less terrifying. She deletes suggestions to hide under overpasses in tornadoes; she changes his definition of a lahar, too movie-esque.

It relieves Brooke to be at work. It relieves her to know that there are disasters for which she could not possibly be blamed.

She asks her husband one evening at dinner, after he has finally had two job interviews, are you afraid?

It comes out like a challenge, and she finds that maybe she meant it this way.

Are you?

No. Brooke pours more wine.

Her husband is rejected for one of the jobs the next day. He receives the email and says nothing.

You'll get something, Brooke says.

Her husband shrugs. He doesn't join her in bed until nearly four in the morning.

The next day Brooke suggests to the head of Volcanothon that they build a town, mimicking their own, at the base of the model volcano.

For scale?

Sure, Brooke replies, kneeling beside it.

This is where their house would be, where her husband had shown her a map latticed with lines and arrows a few days ago and had said, I was asking myself where we would go.

And she said, don't you have a job interview?

And he said, this is all of them. All possible escape routes.

Brooke imagines all of it, the deck where she drinks her morning tea, the bedroom in which they both seem to wrap themselves in more clothes instead of removing them, the living room that in the dark is lit by the watery green glow of her husband's laptop charging. She pictures it all as a photograph, one from the books she read as a girl, the same way she did with her childhood home as it was destroyed: here is before and here is after.

As Volcanothon approaches Brooke reads her husband's entries every night. Sometimes on her own, and she remembers how it felt before the tornado, all that potential, how she hesitated long enough, watching the green-tinted clouds, that her mother yanked her arm. She watched the white bloodless handprints disappear in the basement bathroom, from her fragile skin, in the fragile light, in her fragile house.

Her husband has a second interview for an editing job. He fidgets all night and Brooke marvels at the change in him, his need for constant motion.

The newer entries are not preparedness tips, not how-to lists. Many focus on what to do during a disaster, some what to do after. Like the disaster itself did not even matter, like it was always happening.

Avoid floodwater. It can hide downed power lines and debris.

Curl yourself into a tight ball and protect your head if escape is impossible.

Beware of contaminated food or water.

Be ready to evacuate as soon as possible.

Be ready to evacuate.

That's not how it works, she tells him.

I looked online.

Well, they tell you when to evacuate. You can't just leave.

There's no way they want you to stay.

He is pleading. He is asking something else, something that sounds like a warning siren, like the silence of a hurricane eye, like the cold downdraft before a tornado.

The day of Volcanothon is bright, beautiful. Brooke smooths her husband's Volcanothon t-shirt on the bed where it is a pool of red. Yesterday the software company offered him the job, and she did not expect the rush of relief, how she carried it with her all day and night, the anticipation that he would return to himself once more, that he would be who he was, the same steady, sure man, and she could only be swept away in it as she watched him smile.

Brooke congratulated him, kissed him, but there was a stiffness, something mannequin-like and unreal about him.

He is still distracted all morning, dropping his razor, forgetting the milk in his coffee. Brooke notices how his grin is slow to bloom, but she is in constant motion and they do not speak, not really, until a few moments before they need to leave.

He says, I don't want the job. I'm going to tell them no.

You're not serious. Her body becomes a kaleidoscope, a mass of jarring memories and thoughts and futures all trying to click into place. There is something that keeps him from fitting into the crooks of her arms and the plates of her body and she wonders if it is him or if it is her or if it is both of them, if he is always the slip and she always the strike, if it was the other way in New York and now something has shifted. There is a force and there is an object, there is a disaster and there is an aftermath, and she does not know which is which.

I don't want to do anything else here.

Why?

Even before he shrugs and tells her I have to, she knows. The first time she took him back to her hometown, the tornado sirens screamed around midnight. Her mother and would-be husband sought shelter in the basement bathroom, while Brooke and her father watched the rotation on radar swing north of the city, the cluster of it primal, a fist of deep pink. Her husband was still shaking when they went to bed, and they fucked that night, his fear becoming a deep need— because there was a trembling in him that maybe had never existed before her, a shaking that needed to be stilled.

You're not the same, she tells him simply. You're not the same away from New York.

Neither are you.

He turns, opens the door to the garage. Brooke leaves the kitchen, shocked at the disappointment, hands shaking. She casts around the living room for something to hold, for something to twist, to break.

She tears open his laptop, scans his newest entry. *Numerous hazards exist when you live near a volcano and can occur at any point. Ashfall, pyroclastic flows, lahars—all are possible.*

At the ruins of her old home, the empty lot where she had grown up, he wanted Brooke to say it was horrifying, being underground for those seconds, how it caused her to lose a part of herself.

She did not tell him how she sat there, the porcelain of the bathtub under her bare feet, the radio dimming into static. How her mother shrieked but only once before her terror was too big for sound, that

Brooke could not hear her own thoughts as it happened, and was, for a second, only the tornado, the hook of breath, the white knuckles, the splitting of her world.

She sticks and unsticks the post-it he keeps over the laptop's camera.

What did you do after, her husband asked once.

I don't remember, she'd said.

And she let her head rest on his chest, let him think that she needed comfort. Even though for her there was really no after, only stepping out the door into a world newly cracked open.

She deletes the disaster preparedness guidebook. She deletes all of it.

At Volcanothon they do not speak and her husband seems looser. It is supposed to be his job to press the button for the scale model's eruption, to begin the march of molten liquid. But in the moment he hesitates. He squints. He turns to Brooke and asks, is that our house down there?

It was too much, the tornado, too much but not enough. All at once she wished it had not happened and wished the destruction had been greater.

She takes the controller. She tells him yes. She starts the eruption herself.

7

How Cities Are Lost

*As a child spiders with veins in the womb, so a
woman's mind weaves routes to other places.*
—TOWN PROVERB

Angkor Wat

My mother's ghost peers around corners. Carved stone faces become
hers. Waves of moss over walls become stubble and the torso-thick
roots clinging to collapsed ceilings and doorways are me, clutching
my mother's unshaven leg. I am young in this final memory of her,
and I beg her to take me with her. Her voice is a roar; she is all
tilled-earth hair and forest fire motion.

My tour guide says, ma'am, you look lost. He smiles, lips flaky,
and grabs for my map, my mother's map, folded so many times it is
skin-soft. What can I help you find?

Can you find someone I haven't seen in twenty years? The sun
soaks the temple, its walls and upthrust stone walkways and crumbling
pillars. The scent of decay drapes among vines.

Oh-kay. He drifts away to a man staring at a statue.

I wondered about my mother, pictured her entwined with the swathes of rainforest and desert sands that shrouded the lost cities she spoke of, the ones she marked on maps papering the study walls. This was her manifestation of our town's supposed disease, the wandering insomnia that found women during or after pregnancy. The sleeplessness, the all-night pacing; these symptoms awoke late in her, around my fourth birthday, as though she had created them. Although I heard fevered scribbles in the night, the tearing of book pages, lamplight pooled over scattered papers, my mother was tranquil, unlike the other frantic women. Organized. She did not shout when my father forbade her leaving. He told her she belonged to us, not the world.

She told him he was lucky it took the disease so long to awaken in her.

In childhood I chose to think she could not stop, that it was disease alone, as the men always told us about the insomniac women. I invented games in which my mother hid behind every stooping olive tree, every vine, and in my mind when I caught her she held my hand, our riverbeds of palms cupped, and I knew my spidery unease, the thought that she had left by choice, was false. The boy who became my husband followed, mimicking my motions, chasing not a memory but a childish phantom. Because for him, for all the men left in charge of our town, it was only a game.

I want to find her, I want to ask her why. If she wanted to go or if she had to. If the lives of cities or women are lost by choice or by constant decay.

Mohenjo-Daro

I meet a group of old women in a desert town. I ask if they have seen someone who looks like a fallen city and they ask me for a picture of her.

I have none.

One of them says, she must look like you. We'd remember her.

I have tried to draw her thousands of times, every time I hold a pen. My father hoarded photographs of her, never told me where they were. When I try to trace her features I get as far as pillars of legs collapsing into sand, brambles of hair, domes of eyes half fallen into the sea.

The women offer me wine that tastes of my husband. I tell them this.

One of them says, dear, doesn't everything?

They wish, says another.

The same woman asks, after topping off my glass, where are you from? You look at home here. She has ocean-rift wrinkles, reminds me of my mother-in-law.

I drink and the liquid brims with deep sadness. I reply, a town without mothers.

And are you a mother in this motherless town?

Some believe asking that is a curse. As I say this the wind ripples sand around my feet.

Not all women know the disease will come to them, the insomnia, and I have long wondered if they feared or welcomed it. Because of this, whether the disease is real or not, abortion flourishes in our town.

I tell them, the first time I was pregnant I was afraid, newlywed, and my mother-in-law helped me.

They clink their glasses.

I do not tell them how instead of feeling like an extinction, as I had been told it would, I felt clean. The remaining women of the town surrounded me, dull as dead leaves, crumbling from the detritus of men, of children, of accusations and fear. All of them lost.

I explain to the old women, with their crinkled-vine bodies, how my mother-in-law raised her own boys and the boys of her sister. How I came to her weeping when I was eighteen and she snatched some bitter olive wine—here, drink quickly—and dragged me behind her, all the while muttering, my son, idiot boy. How an hour later I drank pennyroyal tea at her table and her hand remained centimeters from mine without touching. She said, some women die from this.

I did not care.

The women meet my eyes. But they blink suspicion.

Do you have doctors to diagnose this disease? And how does it pass over some?

It is in our blood, that is all we are told.

You have always been told, one asks. So it is all true?

I only know that when women flee, we are left with what men tell us.

As the sky dims the women speak of the lost city that sprawls in the desert a few miles in the distance. It was a planned city, with bathhouses, single-family homes, parallel roads. Traders, merchants, architects. They built a city with a marketplace, with waste disposal, but without walls for protection.

They say, things are lost only by choice.

My mother told me it was a flood.

Whatever it was, they did it to themselves.

I used to wonder if my mother regretted giving birth. Now I am not so sure, because it enabled her to leave.

You told us of the first time, says the one who is like my mother-in-law. Now tell us of the second. Why?

In the distance the Citadel of Mohenjo-Daro, pale against the darkening sky, looms. It is almost like the half moon, pocked with craters and fissures, on the night I told my husband I was carrying his child, just months ago. He kissed me and said, our son will be so brave like his mother. I'll tell him after you're gone.

I say, the remnants of wine soft and silken, dusk and summer, on my tongue: a choice.

They laugh and the air of the dead city wafts over us. The women embrace it, this kiss of bone dust.

Thera

I dream of the Underworld rivers, their names charcoaled on my lips: Cocytus, Styx, Acheron, Phlegethon, Lethe, the river of forgetfulness, the stream of oblivion for which I am named. My mother is there, bitten apples of eyes and stillborn hair.

I learned early to ask my mother-in-law about my own mother, away from her husband.

That woman, my father-in-law said. Those women who leave. They make a choice.

After I had been married for a few years I began visiting my mother-in-law when our husbands were in the olive groves. She made tea and while the steam curled around our hands I asked questions about my mother, a restlessness beginning I could not define, one similar to the wonder I felt when tracing my hands over the photographs of Thera, Ctesiphon, Persepolis.

I asked what rooms felt like with her in them, how her hair smelled, the voice she used to speak of me and why she wanted me and if she ever wept. I could only imagine my mother as she was the day she left, the pillar of a faraway wasted place.

You know, she said, I have often wondered what your mother saw. What she sees. She spoke often of lost cities, what it would mean to visit them, places captive of time, trapped by sand and stone. Even before you. She looked at you, after you were born, like you were a myth. A legend she was told but never believed.

A suspicion, a thought to add to my own—that my mother's disease was a fabrication.

Outside a dog barked. A car sputtered down the gravel road.

She whispered: I think sometimes how I wish I had gone with her. She has seen so much of the world. All its bones and wounds and scars and I wonder if they play out more beautifully than on a child.

I thought of my father, who called me his river of forgetfulness, as though he wanted to wash something away, and my husband, who wanted to hold something of me forever in the form of a child.

That night I snatched my husband to me the way a vandal snatches treasure, the words of my mother-in-law clear; his body felt like smoldering houses, decimated fields, the ruins of places to leave behind.

Nhouadhibou

The ship graveyard smells of rust.

On my mother's map this cemetery of vessels is a pinprick. Before she left my mother gave it to me and said, you are a person carved from want and need, Leitha. She wrapped her arms around me and it was the tumbling of empires.

An old man guides me through wrecks piercing the sand, others drifting offshore. He points to the skeleton of his ship. Says he cannot sleep anymore because stillness awakes in him such fear.

I fold the map into my pocket, tell him, my mother said she felt me move inside her, felt me eel, felt me stiffen and clasp.

My mother gave me her map one night as she strode across the study. I asked if she was leaving. I felt it in her trembling arms, the broken bone shapes of her words. As though she was torn in half.

I must go, she said, brushing past me, placing a pin into the heart of Mauritania.

What are these places? Can I come?

They are places that must be rediscovered. They are cities that have been lost.

How could someone lose a whole city?

When a city is lost, people mean it was left, or was destroyed, or it simply dwindled out.

I ran my hands over the fallen pillars of Nemrud Dagi, the overgrown stones of Palmyra. They seemed familiar to me, although I was young and could not articulate this. They were like the women who shuffled home from market.

I don't understand how a whole place could go away.

People say lost cities are empty, they have no life. But that is why we find them again.

A week later she was gone.

The old man's hands whisper through the air, caress the mirage of a boat. Do you know why ships are always she?

I tell him: they knew I was a girl because I never stopped moving.

When you were born were you still restless?

My mother said I was never quiet.

Not such a good baby then.

The rusted titans spear the sand around us. Creak lonely and sad and aching. They are fortunate, these corpses, forever at rest.

Herculaneum

In the casts of bodies is pain that is dormant, that sculpts itself into cavities, buries itself under pyroclastic flows.

The man next to me, hat cocked like the strike of an axe, says some three hundred skeletons were discovered along the shore below us.

He coughs. Asks what my husband thinks of Italy.

I tell him, my husband wants to mold me into his arms like those bodies into the mud.

Well he's got a point, honey.

When I do not reply, he repeats himself.

I heard you.

Just paying you a compliment.

I think of my mother and how in order to escape, one had to choose. Choose to leave them behind, the men and the children and always the blame for a thousand small crimes. Locking ourselves away or marrying or not wanting children or wanting them. It showed in superstitions rampant and scared, flaring their nostrils and snapping their teeth:

Wait until your wedding night to lose your virginity or you will catch the disease.

A new olive branch over your bed every month will protect you.

Give your husband a tea distilled from this shrub and he will be impotent.

The light skims over the façade of the buildings and I ask the man if he's seen a woman with skin whose warmth has been milked away.

Who is it you're looking for?

I know I am being absurd, I tell him, it would have been years ago.

He takes my wrist like a broken candle, peers at the circles under my eyes. Honey, you need to get some rest. And—he lowers his voice—really, your husband know you're doing this?

The man with the axe-strike hat walks away, shaking his head when I whisper, our husbands always knew we would leave them.

I feel my husband, his scent of warm olives and dust. The first time we slept together was a giving in, and I recalled the words my mother spoke to me on my fifth birthday before I could understand their weight: do not give yourself to a man, Leitha. Swear to me. He will circle your body with his like the trumpets of Jericho.

I admired those childless women of our town, how they carried themselves with the weight of tree branches over water, collapsing over their chosen barrenness and celibacy, clasping their bird's nest hands. Others who locked themselves away, colored themselves barren and spiteful as poisonous fish. But his skin was so soft, flamed against me. Afterward I wondered why I had not already left this town of my own accord.

When I went to my mother-in-law and told her I was pregnant for the second time, my voice was so harsh I did not recognize it myself.

She asked as she reached for her coat, as though she did not need an answer: what is your choice?

The possibilities stirred, the intense desire always wending and vining itself through my bones, mapworks like tendons and muscles. I knew he wanted children. I knew he wanted a son and would not be dissuaded.

My son is a good man. But he will tumble his love over you, preserve you.

Do you think she's still out there?

My mother-in-law thrust her arm through her coat sleeve and replied, she left you a map.

And so I chose. The pennyroyal, the lie. Because I missed the furrows of the Earth, places I had never seen, the way a mother should miss an unborn child.

Mesa Verde. Ur. Teotihuacan. Leptis Magna.

Reefs and stones and quakes. Places shaped against my fleeting cicada body like my mother's lips, like her hands after a bath. She is nowhere and everywhere.

What do you want, my never-born daughter asks, body a stalk of wheat.

Stone temples and broken buildings and shattered monuments. Each a skeleton lover looping wasted arms of walls around my neck.

I dive to the bottom of a cenote with a tour group. The water is coated with blue, bleeds with it, the color I swear my mother was wearing when she left. There is a skull at the bottom that tells me, it is the dye from our bones.

I say I am sorry, that to drown seems terrible.

After my husband and I slept together, the night I spoke to my mother-in-law, I asked if he remembered a woman from our youth, a woman who miscarried months in and still was sleepless, still wandered away in the night.

He gripped my hand and told me that should I grow ill, I should at least know and believe my son would be safe.

Sacrifice, the skull says. It's not for everyone.

I scramble to the surface.

Sometimes I looked at him and wondered: where does this man think women come from? Does he think only sons are born and daughters erode from the rock? For when he spoke of children he always spoke of boys.

The guide asks me if I'm all right. Almost forgot to breathe down there, she says.

You have a waterbug on your eyelash.

They all look at me as though they have never chased someone.

Sometimes I believe men love us because they feel our skin is ghostly, that they can streak our bodies with comets of their memory and this means they will not lose us, because in touching us they touch themselves.

Vijayanagar. Ctesiphon. Zimbabwe.

My bones turn to ash. I trace destinations across my body in constellations of dust. She is always before me; I snatch at arms of women with hair the shade of hers, with skin like hers.

One woman in my youth took her daughter when she left. Her husband woke and, in his grief, hanged himself. When I asked my father why she never took me with her, this is the story he told. He told me again before I left. It was a week after my second abortion, one I told my husband was a miscarriage, and they stood in our kitchen, one calm, the other flailing. My husband shouted that I was making a choice, that I was killing him.

I took my map, I took my boots, and before I walked out I said: This is a choice.

It is not, my husband shouted.

My father nodded, eyes roving up and down my face. Is it?

I shouldered my bag. Inside was money my mother-in-law gave me the night before. She did not weep, but embraced me.

You will be lost, my husband said.

My father did not look me in the eye but murmured about orphans.

When I was a child I saw the orphans whose mothers caught the disease and whose fathers died or fled after their wives, and I asked them to play hide and seek.

They ran or stared. Their bodies unfathomable and thin and empty. Hunger shaped.

Leitha, my father told me, they do not understand. His hand left soil marks around my eyes where he brushed away my sweaty hair.

But it's hide-and-seek, Papa. What is there to understand?

He tugged my hair, soft. How I wish you would hide, and not only seek.

Persepolis

This place always transfixed me, books opened to this page burying our kitchen table. To be here, leave my footprints, dwarfed by pillars, so near to bas-reliefs of curl-bearded immortals and eternally battling bull and lion, is unbelievable. This was the destination my mother spoke of the morning before she left. She asked, stroking a curl behind my ear: Leitha, do you know why Persepolis was lost?

I tried to remember which city Persepolis was. Fire, I said.

It burned. Then fell into decline.

Okay.

But it was found again. It was rediscovered.

Her body against mine, crushing me to her as though we were two stones in a monument.

The sun dazzles. I have scattered myself, grain by grain, left myself in bones of ancient sacrifices, in murky jungles.

An older woman joins me in front of a bas-relief, sweating and huffing. She moves like she has been here before, like the only spaces she understands are collapsed, disintegrated ones.

I cannot speak, cannot breathe. She is halfway someone I recognize and halfway completely new. I can only know by her voice, if she will speak.

She smiles. Gestures to the expanse around us. Can you imagine, she says, how all this could fade away?

Rediscovered, I reply. I wait for her to speak and feel an exhaustion.

She smiles and the weight of it buries me. She turns, strides away, leaves dust drifting in the sun. The god carved into the stone stares past me, past the woman who picks her way down the stone path, past the sand-colored stones, into the desert. A scar, a deep wedge mars his face. He grins as he always has.

We did not chase them, our mothers and aunts and sisters and godmothers, because perhaps we did not need to. As girls we did not pack our bags and beg them to take us somewhere new yet old, somewhere we could be hidden among jungles and overgrowth, desert and desiccation, somewhere we could be lost and rediscovered too. We find them for ourselves, these deserted expanses, their columns of bone still standing, waiting to be rebuilt, erupting from sand as from a body, as from a shallow grave.

8

Devil's Tooth Museum

EXHIBIT 1: A Good Impact Crater Is Hard to Find

A crater. Just a big, circular hole in the ground, right? Not so. It takes a trained eye to identify the high-pressure, high-temperature rock formations created by foreign impacts: the breccia lens, shatter cones, and shocked quartz. As you travel through our museum, look into the crater. What impact remains can be seen?

The day I went back, the museum was already unlocked. The door handle jiggled in my palm, the loose pebble that begins an avalanche. I played this moment in my head in the six months since Syl died, imagined the scent of earth and heat, the warmth of the displays, how my sister's voice would not be arcing before me, over me. How the dust would swirl in the space behind me, settle where she was not.

I was grateful this was not the case.

The simulator was running, its light streaking, reflecting off the dismal coffin-colored walls. As it shouted over cobwebs, echoed in the dove-gray morning, a foreboding looped itself in my stomach, cold and clammy and wrenching. Not quite a circle, the simulator was built to fit in the center of the museum, with two openings on opposite sides. Inside, each wall played then replayed the video, showing the impact that formed our crater, the decimation. Meteors painted around the outside, neon against the night sky background. The thing was enormous, dense. The announcer's voice echoed.

A HUNDRED THOUSAND YEARS AGO, A METEOR GAVE BIRTH TO THIS CRATER—

I sprinted to shut it off, the extent of my repair knowledge. Because our family owned the crater, built the museum, Grandpa was in charge of maintenance. He trained my younger sister to tinker with the displays, cajole them into starting. It was only through their combined efforts the museum stayed afloat. Now, I feared what awaited me.

Across the museum's main room, Grandpa stood at COLOSSAL CRATERS, jabbing the buttons.

"Didn't you give me your keys a few months ago? The first time I mentioned reopening?"

He shook his head. Eyes milked of color, grayish and damp. Slick like rock under waterfalls, in caves. On the COLOSSAL CRATER display board he lit up the following words: CHICXULUB: SURROUNDED BY CENOTES. PRODUCT OF THE EXTINCTION EVENT THAT KILLED THE DINOSAURS.

A scarlet light bled on the map in front of him, somewhere in South America.

"Can you just tell me, did you open that door?"

He coughed. "Told you. We shouldn't reopen." When he shifted, I caught a glimpse of the spare keys, hanging out of his pocket. A relief.

"I knew we waited too long. I swear, if we have mice."

He didn't reply. Kept his eyes on the display.

We'd barely spoken over the past few months, me cleaning the house, packing Syl's old room, telling myself tomorrow we'd start the reopening process, because what else was there to do? Until it had been weeks, months, until we moved glacially into near-bankruptcy. Until I could no longer stand the silence, the sense that, without the museum, Syl left nothing behind. When I brought it up to Grandpa, he whispered, "Just leave it." Went back to his seat on the porch, across the parking lot from the museum, watching dust whip against the crater rim.

I asked Grandpa to help me, take me around, because he knew I was only familiar with the office, the computers and spreadsheets. He knew I needed to reopen and, in order to do that, needed him.

He refused.

I had no idea how so much dust accumulated since we closed. Crater dust, barren and grayed out with exhaustion, with time and exposure, carried heavier than regular dust. Seeped through our clothes when we were children, left shadows and patterns according to what we wore that day.

Grandpa waved me away. "Do whatever you want."

The grime was everywhere. Tickled my lungs, coated the floor. It gave the museum an eerie stamp of decay as I slipped through the two large rooms and gift shop. Compared to the vastness of the crater before us—the museum perched on the rim, the observation deck thrust twenty feet over the edge—it was tiny, decrepit.

I found a crack edging through a window, dead cockroaches scattered over the floor, dead mice under THE TORINO SCALE, and cobwebs. A bust of my great-grandfather had fallen over, and, when I turned on IMPACT CREATOR, a massive meteor struck the Earth repeatedly on screen. Reopening looked more and more far-fetched.

In the office I examined files, bills, budgets. I tried not to focus on erupting still-frames in my mind, with her hair and her laughing, how exhausting it was to be around someone who loved something I could not understand, loved it more than she loved me.

I came back to Grandpa hours later. He hadn't moved. When I asked if he wanted lunch, he shot me a look of exhaustion and magma and he looked so like Syl that I coughed, that my stomach burned, that I threw up twice in the dingy bathroom where the toilet refused to flush and the soap dispenser fell into my hands.

The fun starts in the atmosphere for our meteor, where friction burns away surface material. As the body strikes the ground, it's compressed by sheer force. Better hope you're not in the vicinity when this happens—you'll be swept away by the widening span of destruction.

When Syl was eight and I was eleven she discovered cenotes in a book Grandpa had given her, the sinkholes etched in the brittle limestone at the edge of the Chicxulub crater. It was a year after our parents died, after we'd been sent to live at the museum, a situation Syl dove into, fascinated from the first moment by the gaping, almost perfectly circular impact crater. When Grandpa told her our family owned it she was speechless, while I couldn't even pretend I cared.

"The cenotes, they're around a crater, just like ours," she said, eyes wide and deep with hunger.

"Uh huh." I'd grown accustomed to their silent disinterest in my life, Syl and Grandpa, how their mirrors of faces nodded at me over dinner, in the living room, anytime I tried to tell them about school or my friends. They sank into their grief together like it was a cavern to explore, walking around the museum, speaking only of the exhibits, the infinite processes of the planet. I stopped following them, stopped pretending to be interested in the destructions they spoke of.

She continued. "The Mayans used them for sacrifices. Human sacrifices. Know why?"

"Nope."

"They thought the cenotes went to the underworld. Xibalba." She shoved her book at me, the cover coarse and brown.

I couldn't tell her it scared me, the darkness, the idea that deep spaces held the dead, angry and jealous and sad, waiting to pull me in.

I flipped the pages, handed it back.

"What if it's true? What if we have them here? I bet Grandpa knows."

She questioned Grandpa relentlessly about cenotes, about the crater, about our parents. What colors did they like, did they believe in God, did Mom like growing up at the museum. What did they expect to happen after they were gone and would she see them after she died.

Grandpa answered her slow and soft, took her on his lap, his wilting, wrinkled skin paled and canyoned, told her of course they loved us.

He took me by the hand later, when I asked why this stuff was so important to her, to both of them.

"It's a phase," he said. "Just go along with it."

I couldn't dissuade her even if I had wanted to, because she was sure if we went out into the crater at night we could find the legendary underworld right there in the Arizona desert.

I couldn't hold her back, couldn't avoid being swept up in her excitement, because there was something different about her, even in pictures, an essential knowledge, a core I was missing. Wordless experiences sculpted into her by years I'd never known or even thought about, a force that carves canyons, shatters mountains, commands ice ages.

She'd lead me into the dark, smile, her teeth and her lips yawning extinctions.

I froze, mere yards from the crater rim, while she picked her way down the trail to the crater floor. Every time, I was unable to move, unable to submerge myself the way she did.

I looked in Syl's eyes after she came back and could no longer see myself.

They reflected only stars, the night, the earth under us.

EXHIBIT 3: The Torino Scale

There's plenty of space debris out there, waiting to blast us into oblivion. This chart assesses those threats, posed to us by meteors, asteroids, and the like. Ranging from a 0 (no chance of collision) to 10 (catastrophe likely), this scale ensures foreknowledge of any disaster coming our way.

I fixed the shattered soap dispenser with duct tape and asked Grandpa if he'd throw the dead mice into the crater. He said no, and if it was so important, do it myself.

I dumped them the next day, off the side of the observation deck, and they spiraled down the crater wall.

The air was thick in the museum, full and empty all at once without Syl's voice.

All the while the simulator. THE EXTINCTION EVENT CAUSED BY THIS—

"Jesus, Grandpa, what did you do?"

"You never unplugged it yesterday. Was already on when I came in."

THE METEOR, AS LARGE AS A FOOTBALL FIELD, DECIMATED—

"You've been so helpful."

"Why would I want the damn thing on?"

I unplugged the huge machine, shaking.

He stared at me. His hands were oily, grimy, and I should've asked him what he'd been doing, even though I already knew.

"I can't do this myself."

A gale battered the window. Something fell off the roof, clattered against the emergency exit. The air conditioning, unsurprisingly, was out.

Grandpa shrugged, turned back to the window. "You want to fix it, you can fix it."

As I walked away I heard some strangled noise and I wondered if Syl sounded like that when she died, or if the water rushed into her lungs too quickly for breath.

EXHIBIT 4: Colossal Craters

....

Tales of destruction can be found all over the globe, from Siberia to Central America. Find some of the biggest, most catastrophic impacts the planet's ever seen on the display board.

....

We used to walk the perimeter of the crater. Syl would rather do this than anything else, and she pulled me along with her. Even in high school she loved it: walking the inner and outer rim walls, whisking her feet along the rocks and sand and scrub, unwilling to disturb even the smallest pebble.

I was seventeen and she was fourteen. I was mad at her because her hair whipped into my face, the wind gusting and the sky swelling with clouds and the rain sleek against my skin.

"Syl, I swear to Christ, if your hair hits me in the eye one more time."

"You'll what?" She scampered ahead, flicked her mane back and forth.

The rain quickened, arrows unsheathed.

"I don't understand why I have to babysit you. It won't kill you to be out here alone."

"Babysit?" She laughed at that, laughed an avalanche. "You're the one he's worried about." She hopped, rock to rock. Each wobbled more than the last. She reached the one directly in front of me, raindrops streaking her face. She put her hands on my cheeks and shook my head. "You'd break your neck without me."

When I slapped her away she lurched, all uplift and lava flow.

There was nothing to grasp. I lost my footing, tumbled, not into the crater but down the outside. Scree stuck to my jacket.

My sister didn't turn until I shouted. Even then, she laughed.

EXHIBIT 5: When the Dust Settles . . .

At this point one of two things will happen: the crater will collapse under its own gravity, coupling with debris slides to form a simple crater, or it can become a complex crater if the central region of the cavity uplifts and creates a massive impact basin.

The next day the simulator was on again.

THE CRATER SERVES AS A MONUMENT.

I shut off the machine and thought, monument to what? Monument to something nobody was around to see?

Grandpa watched. Disheveled, his hair rumpled.

"Have you been sleeping here?" I hadn't heard him leave the house that morning; I hadn't checked around the museum last night.

My mind labored. "Look, if you get here before me, could you just lock the door behind you?"

"Who's going to break in?"

I knelt next to the simulator. Meteor decals rustled against my hair. "You know I have no idea how to fix this, right? You know I'm probably going to electrocute myself."

He shook his head. "Syl could do it fine."

I chose to see this as encouragement and shrugged off my jacket. Next to the simulator it looked like an offering.

Dust peppered the air. Grandpa coughed. "Watch out for those wires. Some are frayed."

"I've got it, thanks for checking." I tried not to think of electric chairs and thrust my hand into the underworkings of the machine. Tangles of wire and rust jumbled against my skin.

I struck something superheated. "Jesus." I yanked my hand free, catching it against something rough. Oil covered my arm.

Grandpa shook his head. Walked away as the simulator sparked.

Outside the sun was vanishing under a blanket of cloud, and dust whipped over the crater walls.

EXHIBIT 6: Destroy the Planet

....

Need to blow off some steam? Use our meteor creator to wreak havoc in the solar system and leave the Earth or any other heavenly body as wreckage. Bonus points if multiple planets are eliminated.

....

The last day I saw her a storm approached over the desert.

"And they say it never rains," she said, stiff and unaccustomed to goodbyes.

She was leaving for Mexico, where she would be mapping the cenotes along the rim of the Chicxulub crater. When she told us she'd gotten the job, her shrieks echoed and she danced Grandpa around the observation deck, their bodies rattling and creaking the entire thing so hard I thought we were doomed to collapse.

The moments evolution-slow. I told her to be safe and she stood behind her pile of mismatched suitcases. Some of them were mine.

Grandpa, hugging her. "I'll have to take care of the place myself."

"Alex isn't going with me, you know that, right?"

"Now you're gone, she'll hole herself up in that office day and night."

She laughed. Hugged me soft and tight like the breathlessness that happens underwater and she said, "God. This is stupid. I'll Skype, I swear."

Feeling her bones, granite against mine, knowing she wouldn't call, because she'd see the sinkholes and forget there was anything like a desert existing in the world.

EXHIBIT 7: Great Balls of Fire (in the Sky)

Bolides are fireballs that streak across the sky, causing sonic booms and bursts of light. So take note: Don't let yourself fizzle out. Be a bolide!

The simulator got hoarser, lost focus.

Dust settled overnight no matter how I scrubbed during the day. I came in every morning to fallen posters, peeling decals, displays with pieces missing, wires rearranged. I tried to fix them as best I could. I killed the carpenter ants in the gift shop, put up the fallen shelves. Tried to stop the bolide on GREAT BALLS OF FIRE from blinking like a Christmas light, but without guidance or any knowledge whatsoever I was lost. I tried a different tack with Grandpa, though his opposition to opening grew every day. I was pretty sure he was the one who destroyed the gift shop shelves and detached the display wiring.

"Think you could give me a hand today?" The coo of my voice rippled off the walls. Syl would have only raised hers and Grandpa would have done what she asked.

He snorted. Stood at COLOSSAL CRATERS. The scent of mold, of dusk, shrouded us.

"Dust this display? That's all."

He gripped the rag. Turned back to the board.

I thought, okay, this is progress.

Syl polished the displays each night after close, vacuumed the entire museum, and never had to ask for Grandpa's help. From the office I'd hear them talking about where she wanted to travel, what craters and extinctions and formations she wanted to study.

Behind me, a soft thump; I turned around and the rag was on the ground, already dusty from the fall.

EXHIBIT 8: What's So Great about Devil's Tooth?

......

The near-perfectly-circular Devil's Tooth Meteor Crater can be seen from satellites, from space. As you can see in the display above, or in any of our merchandise, we're distinct. We're proud to say this impact spawned an extinction event, helped give birth to the world we know today.

......

When Grandpa was in the office finishing the reports after close, Syl and I played hide-and-seek.

Syl always knew I'd nestle under Hubble's bust or in the broom closet behind ALIEN IMPACTS. She took forever to unearth me. Sometimes I'd get so frustrated I'd jump out and chase her down, find her wandering, her feet so slow and soft she didn't even scuff the carpet.

She'd look at me with tectonic eyes as though she had to form the words into being, create new matter to speak to me, as though she'd forgotten entirely about me in the face of the displays, the meteor remnants and photographs and endless geology.

When my turn came to seek her, it took me about ten seconds.

She'd be in the simulator. On the floor, curled up, the glare of destruction reflected over her.

Even though our planet has seen its share of mass extinctions, the United Nations doesn't have a response plan in place for such an event. Experts believe the likelihood of a deadly impact is very small, at least on a grand scale. So don't worry, fellow earthlings. It seems the worst is behind us.

The days swarmed in fogs over the crater, in apocalyptic storms bleeding out over the desert, in epochs and simulator shouts. THE METEOR BEGAN IN SPACE, the announcer reminded me.

I re-memorized the speech for tours of the rim, recited it as I cleaned with haphazard fury, but memories of Syl drifted in. I pictured myself leading the tourists, their cameras pointed across the gulf, slanted against the body blow of wind.

"My ancestor, Ernest, was led here by Native Americans and thought this was a volcano—did you know when my sister was hungover she ate fried mushrooms and scrambled eggs—and he tried to make it erupt. Set dynamite charges just over there. He waited and waited. He built his house here. Raised cattle and all the while kept watching—I think about how the last thing she saw must've been her hands, all pale and starred in the sediment—and, finally, a hundred years later, a team identified this as not a volcanic crater but an impact crater."

I spent nights in the office, where I said I'd be going over spreadsheets. I woke up in the dark, neck cricked, to Syl diving into the mouth of a miles deep cavern over and over.

Grandpa stalked the museum. Stayed until after it was dark, until I locked the doors. Sometimes I repeated the speech to him, or counted down the days, but all he said was "Okay" in a voice that was almost a ghost. I took away his keys when I found him unscrewing a display case and removing the meteor fragments inside. He told me I should let the place wither.

Useless knowledge, a grainy mass of debris, built up, lodged in dust particles in my pores. It shifted when I touched anything or moved against a memory, harsh and swift and slippery to the touch.

She drank red wine because it colored her tongue bloody. She loved her first boyfriend because he was a planet she could impact in melted touches, because his eyes were the colors of deep earthen places. She named our dog Valhalla after the crater on Jupiter's moon. When we were in high school I couldn't find my contacts case and she gave me her glasses, then went an entire day without seeing clearly so I could take a Trig test and hang out with a boy whose name I've forgotten. I aced the exam and the boy kissed me for hours, slid his hands over my body with the ease of a strike-slip fault.

She went to the Yucatan Peninsula to study the crater that killed the dinosaurs and went diving even though she wasn't good at it and that's it, that's all.

I thought, there should be a way to destroy these things, burn them off against the atmosphere.

EXHIBIT 10: Alien Impacts

You might find yourself asking, why are craters on other planetary bodies so much easier to see? Take the moon: its lack of atmosphere allows impact craters to form and linger for eons after their creation. We earthlings don't have this luxury of time.

I asked Syl once, "Why craters?"

It was after her college graduation, and we sat on the exit stairwell of the museum that led into the crater, champagne bottle skidding across the metal walkway as we passed it back and forth. The night cool. She hadn't wanted to go out, like we did after my graduation a few years before, when we'd gotten drunk at a bar and walked home through scrubby cow pastures, me tripping over every hole in the ground and Syl laughing the whole time, unscathed.

When I asked her why it was craters she loved, she twisted her pinky in her mouth. "It's like being inside a fingerprint. Like you're part of something's genes."

My head throbbing with booze and wind and eerie whistling

dark. I giggled. "Jesus H. Christ, what does that even mean? Are you talking about Mom and Dad?"

Her eyes dark, Xibalba dark, she laughed and said, "Like, being inside something besides yourself, something that's better and so old."

I shivered. "And it doesn't scare you at all, the fact that it's, I don't know, deep?" I had majored in accounting because it was not empty and scarred, it was not crushing or destructive. What I had learned from the crater, from my sister and my grandfather, was that destruction could not be fully quantified, that extinction could not be fully measured, except in the shock of empty air and shattered stones the color of loss and the sense that right there, right on your shoulder where someone touched you once, or where you hugged them the last time, was a perpetual vacancy, a dark massed point, a hollow that never eroded.

I didn't tell Syl this. I never would, because I knew it was just another thing my sister would never understand: that destruction had never been beautiful or fascinating.

"Who's not making sense now?" she asked.

"I mean, it's bigger than you and ancient and how can you want to understand it?"

What I wanted to say was, how can you look for answers you'll never find? How can you search an emptiness that will always be empty?

She laughed and laughed. Until I laughed, too. Until the night wasn't so deep.

EXHIBIT 11: Potentially Hazardous Objects

....

A P. H. O. is a body with an orbit relatively close to Earth that could cause significant regional damage if it struck. These objects, though they sound threatening, are too far away to be of concern, as you can see by NASA's tracker.

....

A week into my efforts I found the door smashed in, glass glittering across the threshold under the ticket booth. The simulator spouted screeched lines, completely jumbled.

I entered the main room, found Grandpa struggling with the simulator, control panel thrown open. Tearing, gasping, the sounds of some cataclysmic struggle. The machine jerked, spasmed under his fury.

I ran. Shouted. He was trying to destroy it, trying to damage it so irreparably that even he could never fix it.

I tore at him but I was shoving at something as obstinate as the Earth itself, the walls of the crater, my sister, and her undying belief that the Earth held her answers in its veins.

The simulator wailed. Whispered. Screeched again.

METEOR

stayed

IMPACT

Earth

FOREVER

He finally pulled back, oily up to the elbows.

I stood above him, panting. I shoved him and he tipped, turtlelike, onto his hip.

FOREVER

Grandpa whispered something that sounded like "Yes."

The air rumbled.

EXHIBIT 12: Extinction Coming from Afar

The Chicxulub impact in the Yucatan of Central America, according to most scientists, killed the dinosaurs. On the display, piece together the results of this catastrophe—which species survived?

When she called from the cenotes, the last time I spoke to her, she said, "I'm so tired, Alex. I'm exhausted."

We hadn't spoken in weeks.

So I said, hoarse, "Living the dream."

"You wouldn't believe it here. It's so humid. My hair's a disaster." The jungle through the phone, an enemy creeping in. "We've got about a million cenotes to map."

I tried to reassure her. "You'll feel better after you've looked at them. Haven't you been doing that, though?"

Her voice cracked. "Yeah. I'm diving tomorrow."

"They didn't train you for that."

"They're telling me I shouldn't. But these things. No wonder they thought this was the underworld. They just never end. It's like a trail of memory, where you start thinking and can't stop and the finish has to be down there somewhere, but how do you know if you don't see it for yourself?"

I said nothing for a beat. Two beats. Enough beats for thunder to roll outside. Thunder that became the sound of Syl's feet, pounding against the crater floor as she left me behind, as she searched for something the Earth clasped to itself.

"So do it."

Silence.

"I was never not going to."

I told her goodbye. I handed the phone to Grandpa. Heard him say, as I walked away, that she should do it, of course she should. The two of them fitting together, the first moment of a meteor strike, the first millisecond of impact, when a body is cupped to the Earth.

EXHIBIT 13: Experience the Extinction

....

With this simulated wave of destruction, stand in the midst of the Devil's Tooth impact as it happened in prehistoric Arizona. Feel the blast and see the flame—go extinct!

....

I have no idea how long I sat, display lights stirring my shoulders. The air heavy and cluttered. My breath was clotted and I felt like I was drowning.

CRATER, the simulator boomed. Shuddering my shoulders with its force.

Grandpa's hands trembled. His hair a moth wing against the dark.

I told him, the dim scent of Lysol and dirt arcing between us, "You could've done that six months ago."

I turned so I could see inside the machine I was so afraid of in childhood. I used to see my sister in the dark, in the crater outside or even in the simulator, and I couldn't follow her. It was something about the heaviness of the black, about the way it overpowered the sound, the noise, the way she was so small against the violence of extinction.

"We used to play hide-and-seek. Did you know?"

Nod. Like he was remembering, too. Like he heard the palimpsests of her around corners. Like he could feel it, our cemented, limestoned version of her, crumbling and corroding into gaps and festering cavities.

DESTRUCTION.

The light shifted in the simulator, splayed across our faces, the meteor curving hot and sharp and knifing toward the Earth. It had been replaying this way, repeating the strike. When I was little it was real, scorching, and I wanted to warn my sister that it was coming, that it was the end, her hair painted with firestorms.

"She was terrible at it," I said. "So bad. At both. Hiding or seeking."

Grandpa's skin curved like the horizon when I pressed my fingers into his palm, gripped his hand, cool and dry. He squeezed, soft.

I wondered what it was about the emptiness under the Earth that she loved so. Why she wanted so desperately to excise its wounds like they were her own, to make its loss hers.

LET'S WATCH.

A smash circled us, grasped us.

DESTROYING—LIFE—VICINITY—

A cataclysm, the air vibrating. In the panels, across the glass cases, the swarm of colors perforating the dark and in the tremors Syl, her imprint a shatter cone, a remnant, a brokenness that inhabited the innermost hollows of the Earth.

9

The Supernova of Irvin Edwards

Case:

The memory belonging to the human Irvin Edwards flees, wraps itself in gravity, a film of dust and pollen, the skim of a first kiss. It dissipates, unwilling to be terminated; we retrace, watch its molecular cloud beginning, as we have hundreds of times.

We see Irvin Edwards and a girl, both sixteen and golden and fluid, drive to a field in his father's Galaxie. This girl's skin, so soft and warm, awakens in Irvin a fear that his fingerprints will melt into her cheek, mark her forever with his touch.

The sun perches atop a hill in the distance. Trees bristle around them, windbreaks, so livelihoods will not blow away, shatter grain by grain; everything is ghostly through the haze.

They slouch in the dirt, tiny pebbles sticking to their clothes, dead plants crunching under their bodies. The girl says, the world is so round here, can you feel it curve? Like the Earth's pregnant. Irvin nods; she runs her fingers through his hair. They tickle his scalp.

The humidity dissolves her makeup into her pores, streaking Irvin's skin.

As the dark closes up overhead, the cicadas preach *wheee-er*. The ground warmed by two young bodies, feeling how the stars suffocate and their unconscious suicides cannot be seen until millions of years afterward.

We who are not human have watched the species' cycles, traced their memories from afar. With our minds previously unburdened of selfish concerns we absorbed, recorded them, the experiences not our own.

We peer, now, into an emptiness more frightening than the births of black holes. It is the emptiness of worlds that have known life. We study Irvin Edwards because Irvin Edwards has been betrayed by his mind, as we soon will be by ours, which blight with rot, cloud not with our own recollections that will slump away, but the recollections of those we have watched.

We would have previously stated this malady does not concern us. That we merely observe Irvin Edwards; that we feel no pang as Irvin finds he cannot navigate the opening of a Christmas present, or as his children become confused in his mind, or as he wakes up to shower at three in the morning and his wife discovers him sitting naked on the bathtub's edge.

We digress. We must discern why the memory shattered into broken-bone shards. Why, upon the final decay of Irvin's mind, did this memory escape? Fear of destruction? Sorrow?

Or maybe it is Irvin himself who allows this memory, among billions of other memories, to continue. To clutch pearl-strands of other remembrances to itself.

Background of Subject:

(*Note:* We apologize; our haste has forced us to preclude proper order.)

1. Irvin Edwards was created by an army sergeant and a biology professor. They had not only Irvin, but three other children. The army man was dishonorably discharged.

2. Irvin saw his parents smoke cannabis once, twice, many times. He also smoked cannabis many times. It slowed his mind, made him replay how he watched *Miss Saigon* for the express reason of perhaps being seen by his brother's girlfriend. How he drowned an anthill and watched the tiny beings scurry in panic from the mouth of the watery volcano; how they were so small he could not think of them as living creatures. How his eyes had burned in the wind at the cemetery where they buried his godfather, a man who gave Irvin books about the planets and the atom bomb and the furthest reaches of the world, which he read under his covers with a flashlight.

3. Irvin Edwards watches the stars from Spain, London, Poland, Sweden, after he is married; he carries his small telescope, a wedding gift, leaves it in his wife's bag as they travel, tells her it is because she holds his belongings closer than he does. They keep track of the sky together in the moments their travels allow.

4. When they go home to the middle of the country, she attends university. He continues to fix cars because he wishes to be a practical man, but he still attends to the sky; his wife learns of areas where light cannot escape, the weight of ideas suspended in space, the density of a thought in a vacuum. She teaches Irvin, loses both of them in a universe of explosions without sound, decay without scent.

5. Irvin looks at his wife, the theoretical physicist, with the wonder of a man who brushes against the secrets of the universe. Sometimes he does not feel he needs a telescope to view the bodies above them, that they will blur and unfocus and it will sit unused, smelling of Jupiter and Neptune and Pluto. Other times his wife must work late, leaves him with children he puts to bed. Irvin races to the bedroom, pulls out the telescope in a darkened, silent house, comets in his bones and stellar evolutions in his blood, fears that he is drifting further and further away from the mass

at the center of his galaxy. He feels that something has begun to shudder inside him but he does not see as we see: the collapse of a core started, the exhaustion of fuel.

6. His wife frames a photograph after the first round of doctors. After she has held his hand during the spinal tap. After she has pushed his still-thick white hair back the way he loves. It is not a photograph of them. It is from the human telescope. The so-called Ultra Deep Field Image, a photograph of the universe's childhood. She places it on the wall next to their bed, takes his hand, his skin a thinning atmosphere. Says, Irv, you remember this picture I showed you last week? How you said it made you think of me?

He nods. Mmmhmm. His mind flashes pinpricks and spirals.

Her smile is an edge. She is afraid the universe, like her husband, will one day forget how to tie its shoes or what the word for *yes* is.

7. If we could tell them we would say: Some stars go supernova, as Irvin and his would-be wife spoke of in the field that evening. These stars do not take dying lightly and their particles leave the body behind, paint new latitudes. Others, we have observed, do not struggle. They swan dive into the dark and leave a soon-extinguished ripple. These are black dwarves; their lifetimes are longer than the lifetime of the universe thus far, and humans can only theorize what they will be like.

8. We digress. We fail. We have never grasped hands with someone; we have never spoken of unknowable mysteries. We have had no need to become this type of conduit, to replay the movements of Irvin Edwards and his previously stated memory, traced along our untouched tissue paper skin.

Evidence:

Again we see Irvin Edwards's memory, cradled like the ashes of a loved one, beginning to drift. To flood. Irvin's fragmented memory deserts him in the way atoms desert a dying star.

FRAGMENT 1: This pinprick of memory flits through nightmares, lodging afterbirth-slick in the throat of Irvin's almost sleeping wife.

It is fusion, the relics of half-ideas. Bloody-eyed demons. It relishes remaking itself, dragging back into wakefulness, the recognition that the hallucination was never real, or perhaps—

FRAGMENT 2: A splinter of the memory is part of a boy. The great-grandson of Irvin Edwards. His mother tells him story upon story of her grandfather—a man he can never meet, not truly.

Irvin lived a life, the boy's mother says. Let me tell you. The boy asks, tell me what, each time, in a tone of longing as he pictures the drooping, blank old man. She tells him, Irvin met your great-great-grandmother when he was fixing her car. He dropped out of school, have I told you that? He traveled with great race car drivers. He took her to Mexico, to Rome, to Spain and England and Brazil. The boy asks why. His mother shakes her head with continental drift exhaustion, slow and crushing.

FRAGMENT 3: Without a mind to contain it the memory is a word on the tip of the tongue; it is right there, right behind the shoulder, a whisper.

FRAGMENT 4: An ember burns tobacco holes in a retired priest's lungs, the brother of Irvin Edwards. He sprawls across his unmade bed, pictures a sinkhole in the middle of his father's cow pasture, one he saw when he was young, with a bloated bull carcass floating in the fetid water at the bottom, so far down, so deep like the edge of the universe, the edge of space.

Note: The two had been close when they were young, but his jealousy grew when Irvin married the woman he also loved. He never married, never loved any woman except for his high school girlfriend, whose skin warmed the fingers of Irvin Edwards in a field when she should have been faithful to him. Whose perfume he believes he can still smell in the cobwebs of his apartment.

FRAGMENT 5: The wisp claws at walls, whispers through static in deep windy voices, cracked and fading. It loses itself in the dark-eyed ghosts of abandoned farmhouses, who are famished and lonely and miss someone to the point of hatred.

FRAGMENT 6: The memory's dust sifts through the fingers of a man at his wife's grave and mimics the shape of her lips: *We met in Greece, we toured an empty volcano, isn't it reassuring how the Earth dies just like we do?* The memory hollows itself out, becomes an extinct crater, an empty sepulchre for the Earth and for the man and for his wife.

Note: This man went to school with Irvin Edwards. Their sons played baseball together. The two shared many beers and stories already known over uncountable hours in the splintered stands; they drove home in cars always covered with ballfield dirt, each finding a film of the stuff on his tongue and over his cheeks and in the valleys of his face. Each saying in his respective shower, dammit, this stuff gets everywhere, watching the reddish water snake through their respective drains.

FRAGMENT 7: The calcified memory lodges in the sons of Irvin Edwards, unremarkable men of average size and intelligence who do not care deeply for much of anything.

Note: Irvin and his wife spoke often of these, their products, and we have seen the skin gnawed away from Irvin's lips as he contemplates their lackadaisical minds, their drooping smiles. Even as Irvin forgets who these men are he holds a pit of worry in his gut, one that has no word.

FRAGMENT 8: This memory splinter exists as the inkling a one-time aspiring artist never painted. It traces across her eyes in a summer sunset she never saw; she focuses and the flare disappears. This woman never became an artist, instead married a man who kept large coffee table books about the Louvre, which she flipped through every day after vacuuming; her hands, still dirty, left smudges on each crisp page, smudges that had the appearance of small animals frozen in the snow.

Note: This woman is a sister of Irvin. She heard of Irvin and his wife's first kiss in that desiccated cornfield from the girl in question, recalls, each time she visits their home, how her friend's cheeks glowed peachy-pink at the first retelling of the evening she knew she was falling in love.

FRAGMENT 9: The memory lurks in the fogs of Irvin's mother's perfume, clogging her home—the wallpaper, the sinks, the air—with its scent of decomposing flowers.

Note: Each time she returns from seeing her decaying son she runs her fingers over holes he left in his boyhood room, from posters, from darts. She recalls the nights he snuck out and came home in time to help his father with the goats, smiling with the idea that he'd gotten away with his escapes. She bludgeons her mind against these thoughts—Irvin tall and young, Irvin on the baseball diamond, Irvin teaching his siblings to drive—and begs it to shatter like her son's has.

FRAGMENT 10: A miniscule segment of the memory becomes scentless air in our scentless void. It becomes the color of closed eyes, the color of no color at all. It creeps into us, we can feel it. The absence of color fogging our minds. We fear to cut open one another's skulls lest this is all we see: nameless cavities, oily and toxic.

Findings

CONCLUSION: This memory that once belonged to Irvin Edwards, for some reason, will always belong to Irvin Edwards. Has never lost his trace. It will never stop smelling of a teenage boy in a dead cornfield. It will not lose its hint of Irvin's skin, Irvin's chaparral eyes, Irvin's jackdaw laugh.

RESULT 1: Irvin Edwards stores this memory, Irvin Edwards preserves it, and when the moments of his life fade away in marks from an exhausted pen this one goes too, only last. Because it sank into his lobes so deeply, the remembrance Irvin could point to and say yes, this is when I touched her, this is the beginning, when I wanted to be something good and beautiful and lasting.

RESULT 2: Even as the memory becomes a sore tooth, a pocket of pain Irvin does not understand, its motes remain with his wife, a woman who will now look at the people in her life through a snow globe, a souvenir from a destination she never recalls having reached.

RESULT 3: The infinite, endless atoms flood, swaddle themselves in people known by Irvin—as birthdays, Nobel Prizes, introductions at parties, oily engine scents, creatures long thought extinct, lucid dreams and first jobs and last touches and bar fights over nothing—

Predictions

We will continue to watch this lifetime of action, replay it. Exist with Irvin and outside of ourselves until we cannot anymore. We will do so even as we feel an exhaustion that comes from expansion, scraping the universe across itself.

We have perceived the souls of dead stars, black dwarves, and we fear they are hollow.

We know theirs are true deaths, deaths that do not nourish.

We will replay this scene. Create a loop, our own universe in which it is always the last moment, the last time we will remember, like Irvin:

His wife asks him what he thinks. He, mind like torn cloth, will not reply. Will mash his lips into a line, will hunt for words that are extinct.

We see the night our minds spawned something new, attempted to save themselves.

We taste the moment with Irvin Edwards, earthen and grassy.

We catch the growing dark in dustflakes on our tongues.

10

Ashcake

My mom's generation bakes ashcake because they were taught destruction only came for others.

In the dusted morning light, haze creeping across the sun, the island's most revered baker is a force, tuned to something I cannot feel. More than the rest, Mom caresses the dough the way the Earth punctuates its ages, in loving decimations. The bakery doors are open, front and back, and the wind blows from the volcano's direction; the pinnacle stabs the sky while the light chalks, haloed by gritted smoke, hardened, kneaded wisps.

Her twin brother, Obie, grips the counter, his knuckles waves against rocks. Tries to catch her gaze, but her eyes are on her hands, always shifting.

"Come on. Get your hands dirty." She motions him closer.

"Not today."

The dough clings to the cracks in our skin, gray and steepled and rocky. I stir in sugar, flour, cocoa. Just enough volcanic ash to taste it.

She says, "You mean, you don't know how," and grabs a hunk of Kahlua Kilauea from my bowl, rolls it in her palms.

Against the volcano, smoke pours from my uncle's shoulders. His face lit with sky, textured with ocean breeze, almost identical to Mom's but more fluid, less cragged. "No. I mean I can't. Taking the survey team in an hour."

The store smells of ash, chocolate, smoke.

"Those guys need to get out of that observatory more often." Mom shapes the dough into a tiny mountain. Carves a crater into the summit.

"Dana, why don't you come? Should be done before school."

When I was little Mom would never let him take me into open water. So we'd stay at the dock, staring through the depths, making up sea monsters. He'd say, I've seen them, D, how come you don't believe me? It's a whole big world down there.

Mom strides, curls her hand over my shoulder in a surge, powdered sugar and ash tumbling over my shirt. Curls dangling over her face and neck in clouds and strays of smoke. "There's no way they'll find anything."

The ancient eruption, the one from thousands of years ago, left a vast emptiness just offshore, our volcano pillared against the sky just behind it. The void nests there in the ocean; it's popular with divers and dangerous because of the debris, the depth, the dark that seeps over their descent as though from a slit throat. Obie's got a monopoly on the business. Every year he pilots the boat on our class trips and we peer over the edge into the nothingness underneath. We gape above us, then, at the slope hanging over our shoulders, the one our parents love, born of the same forces that mothered the crater below.

I always wonder what we look like from the volcano's summit. All of us in a tiny boat, swallowed by black.

"Mom, it has to go off sometime—"

Obie's eyes glitter, stones just offshore.

A quake strikes. The ground pummels, rocks. Mom grabs the counter.

It's over in two seconds. The smoke above the volcano ebbs and flows.

Obie's breath whooshes. Mom asks if I'm all right. All I can do is nod. They're happening almost all the time now. Usually smaller than that last one. "What're you so jumpy about?" She laughs. "Not going mainland on me, are you?" I can't tell which of us she's talking to.

I smile. The gripping in my stomach doesn't go away.

Mom hates the ocean, has never been on a boat or a plane because she hates the feeling of nothing underneath her. Obie will tell her, yeah, you got Dad's baking gene. And she'll say, what does that leave you?

And he'll say, nobody's got it anymore, the staying away from what'll kill you gene.

Obie hugs me, kisses Mom's cheek, turns to leave.

"They're just being careful," Mom calls.

He walks out and he's shaky through the glass, a shiver of a human.

The volcano doesn't shift, doesn't move. It's sloped, steep, edges stubbled against the growing light.

"Mom. Please. Let me go."

There are times I want to scale it, to say I've done it. Search inside the earth, the cauldron below.

Mom shoves a cake pan at me, the mold's tiny divots craters waiting to be filled, and in this moment putting my hands on something of the Earth seems like it might be a modicum of control.

"Don't be like your father, Dana. Don't believe in things that aren't coming. It'll drive you crazy." She pulls her hair back. "Finish that pan. It'll be busy today."

My generation, we grew up afraid of extinction. Because all of us know how to read the ground, the way the volcano shapes it. I've learned it in school the way we learn how our ancestors worshipped flame and lava. I can recite it without a thought, the way I can the

VEI, the millions of ways a volcano can destroy an island, kill a person, make extinction real.

One day we will fall asleep, leave nothing behind but the space in the air we used to inhabit.

On Thursdays school starts late for seniors. They tell us it's because we need "time to understand our histories" before we graduate, but we already know everything we need to.

Obie's tying down the boat, a big motorboat—I never listened when he lectured about the terms or the names—and when he sees me his guffaw echoes through the deserted dock. "Your mom know about this?"

"Guess."

He shakes his head. The coastline a black snake slithering toward us, as though we can offer it protection. There are only a few gulls circling, squawking, halfhearted. The dock feels eerie. The morning usually fills with seabirds catcalling the fishermen and tourist boats. Above it all the volcano, the crater at the top smoothed into downtrodden horns.

"So? What'd they say?"

"I'm not a scientist, Dana." His words hang hollow in the air, eruptive clouds.

My sides squeeze, pooling and grafting my breath. He's never evasive. "What'd they say?"

"They're worried. But you know that."

More and more people have said good-bye with finality, with tiny explosions. Throwing out things like, you'll grow up to be such a lovely young woman. Or, you'll run this bakery just like your mama. In a way that suggests they won't be here to see. Something seeping into everyone's breath, hardened in their eyes. Making their footfalls, their words, echo. "Evacuation?"

The waves course into the dock and the trees rustle.

"Are we leaving? Mom won't. You know she won't."

Once, when we were floating by the volcano, where the slope meets the ocean and the rocks are always tumbling in, making *plork* sounds with their cavernous bodies, I asked him, why the ocean? We'd gone so he could teach me to dive, and we had watched my mother turn around without waving us away. It was never a secret that my uncle was The Man With The Boat, the man with the escape plan, and it still causes her grief.

I pressed him: people say you're waiting for a reason to run away.

He checked his mask, breathed twice, his voice husked and dry. He hefted himself onto the side of the boat, said maybe they're not wrong.

This is all I think about, watching him. Throwing himself into the belly of the ocean, searching for the depths of something. He says, "Just remember. Your mom and I share the same genes. That means you've got some of both of us."

I tell him good-bye and my feet scuff the wood and I am left walking, holding this bomb of detritus.

School is only a few dozen miles from the foot of the volcano. Around us the palm trees droop, succumbing to the heaviness of the air.

It smells of compacted earth and stone, of crushing and tumbling, of avalanches.

A quarter of us have left. We're crammed into the Volcanology classroom, except Mrs. Maar is gone and we have no sub. Yesterday at the bakery she and her new husband handed their money over the counter and said, Keep the change, Dana. You be smart now.

As a result there's nobody in here to make us watch this documentary, the same one we've watched since we were kids, about all the extinction events that destroy life on this planet. Not even the corny reenactments help this pressure that has built over the past few weeks, since people started leaving.

Nobody keeps their voices down.

"You feel it this morning?"

"Ugh. My stepmom woke me up. She was flipped. Crying in the corner. My dad couldn't calm her down until he promised to take the day off and start packing."

"You think that's bad? My stepdad's in the office right now, yelling at them to close the school."

They turn to me. "What about your mom? Bet she was loving it."

"What do you think? Just went right back to baking. I'm surprised she didn't tell me some legend about how we all came from earthquakes."

"Ha! My mom actually did that. She opened the door—" He mimes the words, stands up.

"Bullshit."

"For real. She steps out into the yard and just stands there staring at it. Then she comes back in and starts going on about our ancestors."

"Both my parents are sure it's nothing."

The ground shivers. I clench my chair until my fingers hurt. The quake continues for minutes and minutes and when it's over the air fills with breaths and sharp pained giggles. Everyone's eyes shift to the volcano, whose top is now invisible through the plumes of smoke. The clouds scuff outward.

"Dana. What about your uncle?"

There is a sound, a shake, like the Earth is mourning. There is an explosion from the volcano that makes the air pulse, makes it harden.

When I was born, Mom says, they gave an evacuation order. Just a precaution, she tells me every year. And Obie will chime in and say, there were mudflows and avalanches, Edy. They told us to leave for weeks before that.

Your father ran away, she will tell me. Her hands over mine, rubble over sand.

"Obie's probably packing." Nobody looks at me. We seize the mountain, clouds swirling in our sight.

The lights flicker. Someone says, "They don't know how to save themselves."

There's this legend Mom used to tell me whenever I was sick or scared, or when the Earth would quake.

It goes: When the island was first formed, when it spouted from the sea, it was empty except for the volcano. And that volcano, it bubbled all the time. Day and night. Slick and orange against the ground, slipping to the ocean. And our ancestors, they were closer to it than we were. They'd hike up to this spot—Mom makes me go every year on her birthday—where the lava cools enough to get close, where it won't set your skin on fire. And what they'd do is burn themselves. See how near they could get. See if they could touch it, could meld with it, could coat their bones and eyes until there was nothing but volcano.

She tells me this story, every time, like she believes it. Like they were right.

We're nothing more than what our parents couldn't keep out of themselves. We're debris, the remains of avalanches.

Thursday is usually our busiest day—Toba Thursday Special, Six for the Price of Four!—but Mom is home, arguing on the phone when they let us out of class early. "Roger, you cannot be serious."

It feels like the day is already eroded. On the way home the air colored purple and thick with rumors, silence on the side streets. It grinds my bones, makes a paste of my lungs. The sky coated with anger.

"Roger, so help me, I am going to do my job and you are going to have the million leftover Pompeii Peaches and Caldera Crumbles leaking from every orifice—" Something passes I can't quite grasp. "Because I know they're your favorite. A little something to take with you, since I can't get in to bake anymore. City council, my ass. Keeping all of us from earning a living over a little eruption."

I start to wonder why they left but we haven't, all of us who are here. Whether there was something they could feel, a certain shift in the Earth or a scent in the soil that Mom just can't get to. Like when I'd push my head too close to her chest when I was little, so my whole world was heartbeat. Which meant nothing was, which meant I didn't have one of my own.

The next morning the sky peels flakes of ash and I hear Obie. "At least let me—"

"How are we supposed to eat if I don't work?"

"Who are you selling to? Where are your customers?"

Their footsteps hail into the floorboards. He grumbles something indistinguishable.

"You don't care," she says, slamming her glass down. "You don't care that you're from here, you don't care where you go or how you live."

The air blisters. "What would've happened if everyone had gone? Nobody would be here. Jesus, you want me to leave, like he did?"

I have never had a father, she told me when I was little. The space where he could be is an extinct volcano, an emptied fissure.

"He was a coward. And all these people who are running? So are they. So are you."

"You're choosing this place, you're choosing a rock in the middle of the ocean, and a bakery that isn't even your own—"

"It is my own. It is mine. I will not let some bullshit evac order take that." She smashes the dough on the counter; it sounds like pumice falling around us.

"No. It's Dad's. It's Grandpa's. How can it be yours too?"

Then he whispers, "How can you choose dead people over your daughter?"

Mom's words slink away, they back out under his fire.

My face scorches and the pain clenches and twists and nooses my insides. My mother and her twin brother are splitting, two halves, their opposite faces bleeding craters of dusk and shadow.

The ash-laden air grows thicker, angrier. There's a scent of brittleness. I look for bags all over the house. All I find are toiletry bags, small suitcases, plastic grocery bags, nothing that can be used for an extended trip.

"Where did you even find all of these?"

"I mean, I don't know. We're getting evacuated—"

She grips my chin, stronger than necessary. "I know you heard Obie yesterday."

"And?"

"Dana." My room grows darker when she sits on my bed. "You'll come back in a few days."

I open the blinds. Everything is haze, eerie. The air swamps in front of the window, muddy and deep. "You think you'll survive this?"

"It's not as bad as they're saying."

"Oh God, what are you, a martyr?"

She sighs. I expect her to say something, anything about how we're all martyrs, all of us who live here, all of us knowing, feeling the time tick away under our skin with every tiny ash grain that lands, every peek over our shoulders at a ghost from thousands of years ago. But she doesn't. "Tomorrow. Pack."

When she would tell me that old legend, I used to ask, how do you know? How do you know they burned themselves?

Now I know why she'd never answer my question. I've always known. It's because being that close to something means our bones, our body, our skin, will one day not be ours. It means evaporation in an instant, in a blaze, in a heartbeat.

"Can't you see what it's like out there?"

She says nothing as she stacks the bags in her arms, totes them down the hall.

"You're a coward. You're all scared. You've been here so long and you're so in love with this thing that will kill you. It'll kill you and it'll still be here in a million years."

Obie always says, only to tourists, because even the kids here know it's a damn sorry lie: See now, folks. Something so cataclysmic, why, it brought us something wonderful.

We know it's not true.

Because our tears are ash. Our footsteps are shocks. We've scored basaltic emblems in our palms instead of veins.

But for all this, we were never like our parents. We know we're filled with marrow and it's weaker than the Earth's.

Mom shakes me but I haven't slept at all, have pretended my eyes are closed against the gloom, have waited for the second explosion they say is coming. "C'mon," she whispers.

I put my boots on, slipping my feet into the crevices without turning on the light.

When I was little I did this, slid them on, ran my hands over the anti-melt soles. Sat by the door and waited for Mom to wake up, heard her rummage around in the dark, stumble into the living room, a smoke spirit. She spotted me just as she was heading out the door, a tiny rock of a person she almost tripped over. Oh Dana, she'd say. Nothing more. She wouldn't tell me no, or maybe one day, or even, there'll be a time when you're older. She'd scoop me up, kiss my forehead, and look me in the eye. I would wake up later in bed alone, and each time it was a mini betrayal, leaving behind imprints, casts.

I can hear my own heartbeat and tiny *fwips* from debris on the windshield. It's a five-minute drive because we are alone on the road.

Everything is gray scale. My reflection against the billowed fog is like an old photograph of someone who is vaguely like me, but the nose is wrong and the cheeks are too hollow and she looks like she's never seen color.

"Mom." We pull into the parking lot toward the base of the mountain. I don't understand how we've made it here without being arrested. Maybe the cops have given up. The clouds look much darker from here, look like they're spreading.

"Need to harvest. We're running low. Have to bake." She turns off the car. "You can stay if you want."

She slams the door.

I grab a shovel.

We drop footprints in the ashy soil. We keep moving forward for something like years until we stop in front of a sign covered with ash. I can feel the mountain over us even if I can't see it.

Mom's forehead soon gets sprinkled with small ash, ash found in dust bunnies under the couch.

She stabs the earth, wounds in such a way that I wonder if it hurts, the scars we are making.

"You want the older stuff," she says. "You want the untouched stuff."

I shovel. "I know."

"You played this when you were little."

"Yeah. Well, I wanted to go with you, but you'd never take me."

"Obie always tried to get you to go swimming but you never did. You just dug up the yard like it was volcanic. Never had the heart to tell you I couldn't use it to bake with."

The ash gets in my mouth. It tastes of smoke and old houses and the emptiness of the Earth when we will be gone.

I want to tell her to come with us. I want to tell her there is nothing here. I want to tell her to choose me.

"When I was little and you would tell me that story, the one about the lava. Is that real?"

We work fast, matching the ash that starts to fall faster. "Nobody knows."

"Why didn't you tell me that when I asked?"

Earthquake.

Mom plants her shovel, hard and sharp, grips as she kneels.

I follow. The pain in my sides empties my breath.

She gives a hardened basaltic grin. "I wanted you to believe me." Her smile is porous and she is leaking out.

When the rumbling starts we have a few buckets full.

We hurry back to the car, the ash sogging to our skin. It makes a paste in my hands and Mom has to wipe hers on the seat before she can drive.

It feels like we've escaped something we can't run away from. We drive on the coast road and can barely see the waves colored with dark.

We look at our home through dirty, fogged glass.

The dark outside is the dark of midnight in the ocean. I'm so queasy my hands shake. Mom doesn't try to make me eat.

Our house is palled.

Obie arrives.

He sees the muddy tracks. He smells the debris in our hair, sees the calderas of our eyes.

They fight and there are no specifics in their shrieks, only danger and eruptions.

My bag has been lumped by the door for the past day but I can't fit enough into it, I don't know how to gather myself into a small space. I slip into the living room, the shouts reverberating in a lava chamber.

Obie pounds on the wall. "Dana, now."

Mom slumps in the doorway, between the kitchen and living room. She is an erratic, left behind by the sheer forces of glacial drift, of lava tides.

Pyroclastic flows bury, burn, destroy anything they come upon. We know, we have always known, that superheated ash melts flesh, that seconds are not enough time to save ourselves; we know our lives can harden around us, can scorch until we are atoms, distilled into a pocket of ourselves.

"I can't." My voice soft, cooling, sagged and empty.

A rumble from both of them, a growing sound that thunders and tears and mourns as it sweeps away. There are too many words to make out even one.

"I can't."

"You did this," Obie thunders, turning to Mom. "You put this idea in her head. You make her think you'll survive this."

"Please, Dana, you have to go. You have to. Please."

The air rumbles. It crashes and burns. My bones ripple. I'm afraid, seeing my mother like she really is. I never saw it when I would follow her into the morning dark as a child:

We are a lonely people. We thrive on destruction.

Obie swears. He smashes his fists into doorposts. Mom is snatching my arm, is yanking me forward and I am fighting, I am scorching at the stories she told with her hands rubbing my flu-ridden young body, the first time she let me bake ashcake alone, the first time we harvested and my skin is tearing and what is left of me is pooling forth and I know, I know what it was for my ancestors to burn with the anger and love of the Earth and the heat on their bodies.

I am screaming. I am begging to stay.

Mom is holding me and we are molten and Obie is shouting and leaving and slamming the door and coming back and the earth is a torch in my skin.

Here is the thing about my ancestors: the volcano, it killed them all. Whether they fell in while trying to scar themselves, or stayed too long, or whether they simply couldn't outlive it. They died, all of them, coated in the cooling embers of something lonely and aching and pulsing under the Earth they could never get to.

There will be no more planes. There will be no more boats.

Mom smashes all our ashcakes. Without a word, her face glimmering in the light. She does it piece by piece, the way she molds them. She has the air of burials. Crater Lake Chocolate, her favorite, makes a dirty scrum against the tile. The crumbs litter the floor.

She slips into the living room, her hands charcoal tinted, already entombed. The residue has leaked into the faults in her skin.

She rests her hands on my shoulders. They dome over my bones and I wonder if by tomorrow we'll be covered.

She walks to the garage, closes the door.

Anything I can say stiffens into glass.

She comes back wearing her volcano suit. The visor reflects gray.

She walks into the dark with a bucket and a shovel and I can barely see her past the deck. A ghost in the ash, a figure I can picture as myself, digging and digging, creating something more catastrophic than a crater. An emptiness where something superheated and eternal, something incubated under the Earth, has leaked away.

11

Experiencers

Q: Have you ever seen a UFO? Give a short account of the incident.

A: I saw lights without a body in the desert, speeding over us. The air was heavy and full and the Joshua trees looked like they were reaching for a loved one who had been away, whose loss was like a ghost, who cannot be seen or heard but felt all the time.

Q: Do you fear long stretches of highway, open fields, empty rooms, etc.?

A: My mother told me, that's when they come for you. When you're camping. When you're at the window. When you're staring at the sky, searching for them.

It is the day after the daughter's honeymoon and two weeks since she saw her mother. Two weeks of driving through Utah sands colored like translucent scabs and New Mexico sunset in pink and ochre and Southwest desert shimmery with water lust.

She crosses to her mother, hugs, but her mother's arms circle without touching, orbit just off the surface of her body. The daughter remembers being a young girl, reaching for her mother who only gazed at the stars.

You camped in the desert, says her mother. All that emptiness.

It was beautiful.

I've told you to stay away from open spaces.

Her mother had been abducted. The daughter was only a child when she found out, too young to understand why her mother did not speak of her trip above the planet, did not go into the doctor's office with her or hold her close on the couch but retreated into her room and made sounds, soft and deep like a wounded creature, when the daughter watched *E.T.*

But I saw something that night, the daughter blurts. Right as the sun was setting.

The daughter remembers the gulf between her and the lights above the desert, how charged for a moment the air was, how loose with relief she felt. In her mother's face she sees, then, the gapping of herself from the sky, the sinew-slick thread she cannot grasp, the tendon unconnected between them.

Her mother stares, appraising. Saw what? Not them.

Lights.

What did you see?

I lost some time, while the lights were overhead.

Tell me, says her mother, haunted. Tell me all about it.

She does, because her mother never once asked her this, not about a test in school or her first job after college or when her then-boyfriend proposed.

They camped in the California desert one night, not far from a decaying little town by an air base. She feared there was always something above her she was missing that darted out of sight just before she looked up.

The Joshua trees scraped the sky with their branches that were broken limbs and she sensed she was being watched, that should she turn around quick enough, she could catch the spindle-armed trees jumping closer. The sky wallowed in unnamable colors, shifting from purple and seashell pink and crisp sky blue into seeping-vein dark, the searing softness of deep fear, and there was something about it like her mother's eyes when as a child she asked if the aliens would take them both, take them together so they could hover above the planet forever.

In the sky, chasing closer, were lights. Three of them, triangular, unblinking. Slightly obscured, foggy in the haziness of evening.

She looked to her husband and back and the lights had moved and she swears she remembers they had no body and she asked, do you see that?

He squinted. Where?

The lights passed over and through long thin clouds that she promised herself were not jet contrails because her mother told her once, pointing to a plane, that the visitors do not leave trails, do not leave anything in their wake except absence.

She pointed. She was clinging to something. She was peeling back the sky.

When she finishes, her mother has held her hand the entire time and the daughter wonders if the touch will be scalded into her palm, a mark she can point to and use as evidence and say, this is a conduit. I have experienced something.

She holds back the end of the story, how she does not fully remember what she saw as the lights sped overhead—whether they had substance, a body. She does know, however, that she never lost time. That she holds every grain of sand between her quivering fingers, every centimeter of empty air between her body and the lights, and how she imagined she was made of iron for a moment, magnetized and drifting up.

Her mother whispers, it must have been awful.

It was fine, Mom.

You should see someone.

The daughter cannot hide her wariness.

He's a hypnotist. He helps people recover what they've blocked out. Her mother gestures to her laptop across the room. Take his questionnaire online. He's an investigator.

The veins of the daughter's hands slide under the weight of her mother's unfamiliar caress.

The mother smiles. You've experienced something. You're an experiencer.

She takes the online questionnaire that night. She takes it in bed with her new husband kissing her neck and sliding his hand down her shoulder blade. Hang on, she says, I'm doing something.

When the daughter found out about these otherworldly visitors who took her mother, she asked questions to find out why and when and what they wanted, if they would come for her too and show her these worlds, these stars. She thought it would draw them together, mother and daughter.

Experiencer, she thinks. Because she's been through something.

After she submits the full questionnaire she pretends she is assaulted by eyes, huge bombed-out craters of eyes, showing her herself in their fullness.

Q: Have you ever awakened to alien beings in your room?

A: My mother stood above my bed some nights. Every time I woke, before I was fully alert, I thought I saw a gray being, a visitor, and I was never afraid. I only felt relief. Excitement. For only a second, before I realized it was my mother. Staring at me. Arms crossed. Like she used to look when she was searching for them.

Q: Do you feel a special influence in your life or controlling force outside yourself?

A: I was a little girl the first time I overheard my mother telling my father that she was sure I was a hybrid. That she waited for them, every night, to give back the daughter she carried before the abduction, the fully human girl curled in her womb. The daughter they replaced with me.

Before her first appointment the daughter thinks of how to get out of hypnosis. She does not need to be hypnotized to understand that she has been through an event that ties her to her mother with helixes and strands far stronger than DNA; she tells herself this, but around her gut, in python-grip tendrils, is the image of jet trails and not clouds against the sky.

She cannot ignore this as she enters the investigator's office and introduces herself.

As she sits down she says, I don't want to be hypnotized.

The investigator's glasses slide down his nose as he nods, cool and serene. He says, it's up to you. But that is why most people seek me out.

There is a knot, hard and oaken, in her stomach. She has tried all morning to reassure herself about what she saw in the desert, even asked her husband. He looked at her, tilted his head, and said, you told your mom, didn't you?

Is it required?

Many experiencers feel it's therapeutic. You may be holding something back, a key to understanding what happened to you in—he flicks through the papers on his lap—the desert. When you lost time. If it makes you more comfortable, we can just talk today. Leave hypnosis until next time. Tell me: What makes you nervous about being here?

She shakes her head. I'm only doing this for my mother.

Tell me about that. Why did she want you to come?

She hesitates, culling words from the air. Moments pass.

I used to hear my mother in her support groups. Explaining how they came for her every night.

She's an experiencer too, then.

The daughter nods, and the motion is too quick and bouncy and she cannot stop the words from bleeding out. She used to say I was a hybrid, manufactured in a lab far away from Earth, implanted, never fully human. A mixture of DNA stolen from her mixed with the DNA of an alien. I told her all the time: I'm your daughter, Mom. You can't give me back because there's nothing to give me back to.

And what did she say?

The daughter still feels the words under her skin. Hears the monotone indifference of her mother's voice, the chill.

All she said was: They tell me I'll miss you.

The investigator scratches notes.

She continues because the sound of the pen reminds her of her mother's fingernails against the tabletop when she pushed away, seeing something no one else could in the lanky body of her daughter, in her long fingers and arms.

I told her what I saw and she wanted me to come.

He does not look away when he says, and what did you see?

Something bright in a darkened sky. Something I've looked for since I was a child.

He leans forward.

She says nothing else because there is nothing else to say, except the real memory, hovering just above, a body obscured by dusk and haze that she tells herself was real, was hiding something new.

Q: Have you missed chunks of time that you have no explanation for?

A: In the desert when I saw the lights. All I remember is seeing them, then they were long past and the night had come.

Q: Do you feel you are being watched or followed?

A: I've always looked at my mother and felt I was missing something, something behind me that she was always watching for; when I was younger I always held my own gaze in mirrors for moments longer than I needed to, just in case I could find it, tell her that whatever she was seeing, I had seen too.

As the sessions go on the investigator insists on hypnosis. Though the daughter refuses, she begins to waver. He stares at her from his skeleton-armed chair with a palpable hungry gaze, asks pointed questions about the experience in the desert. If she has ever had visitations. If they spoke to her.

She is afraid of something that walks behind her, that pounces on her while she sleeps. Her mother asks her when she can come to the investigator. When they can share this experience together. The beings find you at your most vulnerable, her mother says. Hypnosis can help. So you know what to expect when you're sleeping. When you're exposed.

The daughter says she's not ready yet.

That evening at her appointment she asks the investigator, my mom wants to come with me for a session, but that's not allowed, right?

The investigator shrugs, shoulders like earthquakes. Do you want her to?

The wind whistles through tiny cracks at the edges of the window.

Her mother looks at her when she visits now, rather than through her. As though the daughter has foundation and being, as though she is the product of moments and experiences and memories. The daughter recalls how, when she used to arrive home from school, brandishing drawings of houses her mother said looked like spaceships and families she said looked like grays, her mother did not look in her eyes, did not look at her body, but at something far beyond her, something in the depths of space.

The investigator eyes her after she has not spoken in moments. What do you think?

The investigator, on his website, speaks about his own experience. How the visitors came all through his childhood. How they told him, you are special. We have chosen you.

The daughter wonders what it feels like to be desired that way. To have another being select you over any other creation, any other outcome, in the universe.

What does it feel like, she asks, knowing you've been chosen?

He says, rubbing his bald patch, it's like being known.

She tries to conjure images of space and the Earth far beneath her and the voices of gray beings. Strands of empty moments, all stitched together by what she has forgotten.

She is scrabbling at some knowledge she craves.

You're holding something in about your experience.

She stands up, paces, too energized to sit. When I had bad dreams my mother would race in past me with a knife and check the window seals. Once, twice, four times, before she ran out and checked the others.

She was afraid for you, because she was abducted. Just like you.

His voice uplifts on the last word, almost a question.

She feels like she did on the nights her mother saw headlights knifing through windows or heard possums in the attic, when she reached into the daughter's room and snatched the softball bat from her sports bag in desperation. She never confessed that she was awake during these moments, heart racing, that she could not sleep while her panicked mother paced the hallways, relocked the doors, hunted every sound and every wavering light, determined to snuff out every shadow and every nightmare except her daughter's.

Q: Have you ever dreamed you were flying?

A: No, but on my honeymoon I thought for a moment I might be, that the world had spun away, that I was somewhere new. That I'd come back and talk about the world and how it looked as a small drop in a dark sea.

There are days after speaking with both her mother and the investigator that the memory is too much to grapple with, and the daughter is empty, squeezed. She looks at herself from a great distance, from space, and feels she is in danger of unmooring and floating away, into a dark vacuum that is more full than her body.

Her mother asks about the investigator. The investigator asks about her mother, about the visitations, about her own belief.

The daughter feels she is on a table with unrecognizable faces staring down at her.

She takes calls from her mother at all hours, the phone's vibration heavy in her hand, so full it might drop through her flesh, through her bones, because she feels she is drifting into nothingness. Her husband tells her to stop answering.

She finds herself wishing more than ever that the lights above her in the desert had been a haunting vessel, a new body into which she could have been taken.

It is three in the morning when the daughter is nodding off, weightless, and her mother calls. The daughter blurts without thinking, you can come.

That night the daughter dreams of fingers, long spindly bridges of fingers that sway in the wind, and she is on one side of a vast rift, and on the other side is a body, a gray whisper of a body that walks backward onto the bridge and the daughter tries to meet it, strains, but the fingers hook into her body, into her flesh, into her marrow, until she can advance no further.

Q: Why do you believe you were chosen?

A: My father said once when my mother was pregnant she stood in the grass in the middle of the night until the dew sank into her pores. She held the sapling of me in her belly, whispered that I was not hers, that she had not chosen me but was given me by the visitors. That I was half a gray-skinned, long-fingered being with eyes like lakes in the night. She said she wanted the visitors to take me back because I would have eyes like that too. So deep they had no end.

On the way to the investigator the sky is closer than normal, suffocating. To the daughter every cloud is a vessel come to claim her.

Her mother clutches the console between them.

The daughter considers telling her of the memory. She opens her mouth to say that she searches behind every star and always has but she does not know if she has found anything, but each time she sighs until her mother looks at her in the parking lot of the investigator's building and asks if she's all right.

She is on the verge, she is on the edge.

Her mother smiles and takes her hand. This is my fault, she says. If you hadn't been my daughter they wouldn't have come.

She stroked the daughter's hair in the night sometimes but never held her hand. The daughter wondered, always, if it was because she was waiting for them to become slender and long-fingered and empty of warmth, without veins or wrinkles or other signs of life. If every touch of palm to palm became a jolt of memory, became gray flashes holding her down.

Don't be silly, the daughter replies.

Her mother sits back but does not free her.

When they sit in the investigator's office the pit in the daughter's stomach is a great crumbling expanse, a canyon with walls falling into itself, taking everything with it.

The investigator and her mother exchange pleasantries. The daughter feels sick.

Maybe she doesn't really remember, she thinks, the thought desperate and weak. Maybe she really did lose all that time and maybe she is forgetting something and maybe the plane is all some elaborate dream she concocted to cover a deeper memory.

Shall we? The investigator motions to the leather couch and his smile is so bright it is a star through a telescope, the sun through a lens.

If she throws up, she thinks, maybe this will stop. Maybe she can keep lying. She thought of this all night, steeled herself, but she does not know and that is the scary thing. She has done research on hypnosis, from scholarly papers debunking it to websites with lime green font slashed over a black background. They have all said: most people find themselves more suggestible under hypnosis. More inclined to be led by questions. It is this she fears, that the investigator will pull her uncertainty out the way a magician pulls scarves, slithering from her mouth, eeling through the air, slimy and discolored.

She does not know how it will be and she does not know what she believes, and her mother says, I'm so glad we're sharing this, I'm so glad, and the leather sofa creaks, hard and soft all at once.

I've looked this up, the daughter says, far away from herself. I've read it leaves people open to suggestion.

You'll be fine, says the investigator.

He begins.

She thinks of them all, the experiencers who see the investigator because they want to forget what they remember and remember what they forget, who are always burdened by what they know they have seen, by vessels crowned in darkness and brittle fingers and an emptiness so vast no calling can ever fill it. The experiencers are always telling themselves no, it didn't happen, I do not shudder when I see headlights or flinch when I see gray, and when I touch another body I do not lose count of the seconds until I am alone again.

The investigator primes her with easy questions. What is your name and why are you here and can you tell me who I am. She answers and hears the child in her voice, the child who used to tell her mother she hoped every plane winging overhead was a spaceship, would land on their lawn.

Have you experienced contact with extraterrestrial beings?

She grips her mother's hand and says nothing because the words are too sinewy to hold. They are fragments of light, pulsing ever closer but zigzagging away.

What did you see in the desert?

Lights. The words become an oil slick.

When you saw these beings in the desert, these lights, what did you think?

She is back there, back where she will always be, never leaving the moment she stared into the desert sky, telling herself yes, she lost time. She is always in those moments, will be her entire life, those moments in which the lights passed over, when she wished they were something unknown, when she thought not yes, yes, yes, but please, please, please.

SOURCE ACKNOWLEDGMENTS

"Un-Discovered Islands": *Pleiades* 39, no. 1 (Winter 2019): 152–63.

"The Disaster Preparedness Guidebook": *Sou'wester* 46 (Spring 2018): 99–107.

"The Lemurians": *Territory* 7 (February 2018); http://themapisnot.com /issue-vii-liz-breazeale/.

"Four Self-Portraits of the Mapmaker": *Nashville Review* 21 (December 2016); https://as.vanderbilt.edu/nashvillereview/archives/13349.

"How Cities Are Lost": *Arroyo Review* 9 (Spring 2017): 110–19.

"Devil's Tooth Museum": *Flyway*, April 2016; https://flyway.org/fiction /devils- tooth-museum/.

"Experiencers": *Sycamore Review* 27 (Winter/Spring 2016): 76–85.

"Survival in the Plague Years": *Passages North* 37 (2016): 42–45.

"Ashcake": *Carolina Quarterly* 65 (Fall 2015): 12–25.

"Extinction Events Proposed By My Father": *Booth* 7 (Winter 2016): 72–83.

"The Supernova of Irvin Edwards": *Tupelo Quarterly* 2 (Fall 2014); http:// www.tupeloquarterly.com/the-supernova-of-irvin-edwards-by-elizabeth -breazeale/.

IN THE PRAIRIE SCHOONER BOOK PRIZE IN FICTION SERIES

Last Call: Stories
By K. L. Cook

Carrying the Torch: Stories
By Brock Clarke

Nocturnal America
By John Keeble

The Alice Stories
By Jesse Lee Kercheval

*Our Lady of the Artichokes and
Other Portuguese-American Stories*
By Katherine Vaz

*Call Me Ahab: A Short
Story Collection*
By Anne Finger

Bliss, and Other Short Stories
By Ted Gilley

*Destroy All Monsters,
and Other Stories*
By Greg Hrbek

Little Sinners, and Other Stories
By Karen Brown

*Domesticated Wild Things,
and Other Stories*
By Xhenet Aliu

Now We Will Be Happy
By Amina Gautier

*When Are You Coming
Home?: Stories*
By Bryn Chancellor

One-Hundred-Knuckled Fist: Stories
By Dustin M. Hoffman

*Black Jesus and Other
Superheroes: Stories*
By Venita Blackburn

Extinction Events: Stories
By Liz Breazeale

To order or obtain more information on these or other University
of Nebraska Press titles, visit nebraskapress.unl.edu.

CPSIA information can be obtained
at www.ICGtesting.com
Printed in the USA
LVHW090008201119
637878LV00009B/937/P